The Philosopher

Knolan Kemp

ISBN: 978-1-0882-6023-4
Title: *The Philosopher*
Author: Knolan Kemp
Digital distribution | 2023
Paperback | 2023

This is a work of fiction. The characters, names, incidents, places, and dialogue are products of the author's imagination, and are not to be construed as real.

Published in the United States by New Book Authors Publishing

For My Late Grandfather, Douglas Martin.

Chapter One
A Beginning To An End

Staring out into the bleakness of night, the man couldn't decide whether the dusk provided a sense of comfort or fear. The night meant that another day had gone by, yet it held creatures and horrors that could prevent one from seeing the morrow. The man half-expected the talons of a deranged raven or lightning bolt to fly through the window and strike his face; however, the only thing that had come through the window as of late was a chill breeze and a friendly owl that had perched itself in the rafters of the study to observe the happenings of the room.

Amidst his thoughts, the scribbles that adorned the page of his journal had become nothing more than musings and intrigues he entertained during the day. He wrote not to become a prolific novelist but to search his daily life for anything that may lead him toward the holy grail of written literature. The *Book of Knowledge* was out there on some horizon and his worn and tanned hands would surely grasp it eventually. *Eventually* was a strange term used by procrastinators and the driven alike to mean that things were achievable at some point in time.

There would be no true satisfaction in bearing anything other than the book in his mind. His thought process shifted through his recent travels to a market in which he discovered a book vendor who sold books bound in every substance imaginable on every topic one could dream of. The dealer had allegedly seen the book a while back in the town of Havenstein which lay nestled between the Dower and Node Rivers. Havenstein was a bustling town miles away with its towering architecture and plentiful storefronts. That would be a journey for another day, for this one was coming to a close.

The weary man wrote late into the night until his pen nearly ran dry of ink. Words flowed across the pages of the hefty journal consisting of varying degrees of legibility with some being crudely and intricately connected. Periodically, a rudimentary sketch would be drawn of strange creatures that the man observed during the day. Perched above in the rafters, the owl intently watched the man jot down his musings, observations, and prose. The only comfort that existed in the cottage aside from the owl was the glass of amber-colored scotch that sat beside him on his oaken desk. The beverage was strictly savored rather than wasted in an attempt to achieve some materialistic bliss. Everything is best enjoyed in moderation. If one reads too long, the novel becomes a blur of letters and intellectual nothings. In the same light, indulgence becomes a problematic crutch or addiction that the man would rather avoid.

Distilling his thoughts, the man teetered on what some may call madness while others would refer to it as vivid thought. Writing had become both leisurely and therapeutic for the man who once said that writing was a pointless practice of wasting ink. Putting down his pen, the man felt his eyes becoming weighted and decided that sleep was a necessity. The man walked down to the main floor of the cottage, leaving the owl alone in the loft. The man settled into his humble bed and drifted off to sleep.

The morning broke like an egg into a cast-iron skillet. Unfortunately, the man possessed nothing resembling an apt breakfast aside from a couple of slices of stale bread and an apple that had been acquired from the orchard that thrived across the way from the cottage. After consuming what some would call a brief snack, the man put on his black coat and proceeded outside into the cool fall breeze. Leaves crinkled and trees swayed. The crisp air was a blessing in contrast to the stuffy air that lingered in the cottage.

The sun cowered behind a grouping of clouds as the man mounted his horse, Galileo, in his quaint stable. Now seven years old, the black gelding had toted the man all over the countryside and from town to town. Today, the steed was going to fulfill his duties once again by delivering the man to Havenstein. A good horse was priceless to a restless, roaming soul like Braxton.

The duo headed off down the dusty road in pursuit of the town in which invaluable information may lie. Passing under trees and winding through green hills, the journey took a matter of hours before the silhouette of the city came into view with its looming clock tower looking over the rest of the town. The streets bustled with vendors, pedestrians, wagons, and other people on horseback. The wooden wagon wheels rumbled on the rough surface of the cobblestone streets making it sound like a far-off thunder constantly sounding in the distance. The vendors had all sorts of wares, marked up beyond belief, from people selling trinkets to some peddling produce from far-off lands. The smells of freshly baked bread from a nearby bakery made the whole atmosphere a pleasant one with just a touch of urban chaos. Vendors shouted alluring messages and deals while the pedestrians went about their day going in and out of shops and occasionally taking interest in a vendor.

Braxton hadn't been to town in a while, but there wasn't much that changed aside from the seasons and days in a town like this. The storefronts had seldom changed hands from when he was a boy with many passing down family lines. The only alterings that seemed to happen to these storefronts were the brickwork cracking or their coats of paint fading under the rays of the sun. As Braxton proceeded down the street, the aroma from the bakery was replaced with the harsh scent of shoe polish and tanned leather that was being exuded from a cobbler's shop. After a little more distance down the street, Freeman's Pub came into view with its signage and lights that were nearly as burnt-out and weathered as the patrons inside. However, there was no better place to look for a lead than the gossip palaces that these establishments served to be. Plus, Braxton hadn't seen Sean Freeman, an old friend, in ages it seemed.

As soon as he walked through the door, the traveler caught an array of glares, glances, and grins from patrons who either recognized him or seemed to be blissfully intoxicated. Everyone was an old comrade when you wouldn't remember them by tomorrow anyways. After a momentary pause in the chatter and laughter, the cacophony of tasteless jokes, half-remembered stories, drunken knowledge, and clinking glasses ensued. The only person who seemed to still be paying the newcomer any mind was Sean, a burly man in a white apron that covered his powder blue undershirt. Aside from a few gray hairs and a couple of new stains on his attire, Sean looked much the same as the last time the two collided with his fiery-orange beard and bushy eyebrows.

Sean finally put on a smile and greeted Braxton, "Well look who came out of the woodwork. Long time no see there, stranger. How's life on the cliff treating you?"

Braxton was taken back to his days when he and Sean were younger with slightly less natural wear. He couldn't help but smile around Sean. After formulating a response, Braxton chimed, "Life's been cordial with me thus far, so I fear my comeuppance has gotten behind schedule and will have to settle for a later appointment. I see you're still in the same place as I last saw you. How's the pub situation going for you?"

"It's been up and down; however, it isn't much of a bother when you're surrounded by good people, strong drinks, and a healthy dose of financial stability. I've heard some rumblings that you're on a goose chase for a specific book. Any truth to this?"

"Well, yes, but I don't think my endeavor would much intrigue you. You've never exactly been a book nut, my friend."

"The only reason I mentioned it was because a prominent gambler who frequents this place asked that you be shown to the back room."

"That makes things much simpler, for that's the primary impetus by which I'm in town. Is he available now?"

"He said to show you to the back whenever, so I presume that he is such. Let me show you to the room."

With that, Sean walked out from behind the bar displaying his beaten black slacks that hadn't seen a tailor in many moons with assorted scuffs and stains lingering on the fabric. The pair walked to the back where an ornate door guarded what would surely be a fateful meeting between some sleazy poker jockey and a directionless wanderer.

As the door slowly opened inward, there was a poker table adorned with an intricately designed border that held down the black felt of a card playing surface. A few of the faces that sat around the table glanced up to see what had disrupted the tension and silence in their poker niche. The players quickly lost interest and averted their eyes back to their hands where their fates lay. However, the man furthest from the door kept his attention on Braxton.

Kingston Devalve wore a midnight black overcoat over his starched evergreen-colored undershirt. His silver watch tirelessly made its rounds as a cigar hung from his lip like a derelict mountain climber hanging from the face of a cliff. The man adjusted his spectacles upward on his nose to assess the stranger who Sean had brought in. Just as he began to truly analyze the stranger, everyone, aside from the cowardly individuals who had folded, laid out their hands to produce a common verdict. Kingston had won again. Despite the brief grumbling that ensued, the men pushed their chips toward the victor and exited the room leaving the stranger, Sean, and himself as the only occupants of the chamber.

After the awkward purging of almost everyone from the room, the air hung still with the only sound being a faint ticking from the watch that clung to Kingston's forearm. Sean broke the silence, "Mr. Devalve, it's your lucky day. Aside from winning your last hand, the man you wished to see is here."

With this, Sean exited the room briskly and quietly. Mr. Devalve took a brief sip from a glass containing a clear liquid and addressed the stranger, "I was wondering when you would find yourself here, my friend. The name is Kingston Devalve. Fortunately, you've got some convenient timing. I believe I know of something that you want, a specific book of sorts."

Braxton finally broke his silence, "What might a notorious gambler like you know about a book of any sort?"

"Contrary to popular belief, some of us men of odds and luck do know something of books. I know something about a book that not many people know whether or not they have read every novel there is from cover to cover. The *Book of Knowledge* is not something that will simply be hidden in some elaborate Labyrinth or some booby-trapped temple. The path to such a talisman is not one wove through green hills or perilous peaks. Rather, this is an unorthodox journey that will require the utmost flexibility and grit known to man. The thing you seek is located in a place known as Wanderer's Keep. I know not of the whereabouts of this place, so you will have to seek out someone who may help you further in your journey, Ebner Frost. Ebner Frost is an older gentleman who used to wander far and wide, much as you, but he now finds himself in poor condition to travel even out of his home. His hovel is located over in Blackstone above Samson's General Store. Seek out this man and give him my graces, for he may need them sooner than later. And one word of advice for you my friend: don't judge a book by its cover."

With his knowledge all on the table, Kingston outstretched his hand for Braxton to shake. Two people who had been strangers moments ago now knew of something far greater than themselves and the handshake between the two was rather the assurance of a commitment rather than a mere pleasantry. During their interaction, the gambler had placed a green poker chip into his palm.

Kingston explained the chip, "If Ebner asks who sent you or asks you for some proof of good intentions, show him that and he will understand. Keep it both as a memento and a show of my endorsement because otherwise, things may become more complicated and inverted as you proceed."

Now weighted and armed with advice and information, Braxton departed from the pub to the street where mass hysteria ran rampant. The source of the commotion was riding down the road on top of three painted stallions. Bandits.

Chapter Two
An Obscure Observer

The bandits wore crimson bandanas over their mustaches and crooked mouths that only allowed for their cruel, dark eyes to show through their guises. The men carried rifles and blunderbusses that were on display for all the folks of Havenstein to behold. Sacks tied to the saddles of the horses jingled with coins and other riches. Braxton ducked behind a stray barrel as a bullet soared over where his figure had stood only moments before. Vigilantes appeared from around the nearby corner with one of them immediately firing upon the riders. This spark of resistance was quickly extinguished as a bullet collided with one man's forehead making his lifeless form slump to the ground with a sickening thud.

Panic surged through the rest of the group. The remaining vigilantes ran for cover only to have the masked thieves ride off in the opposite direction with their bounty in tow. A few pedestrians lay limp in the streets with blood pooling around their wounds. Amongst the carnage, a cart that once held produce had overturned resulting in a portion of the road being covered by smashed and runaway melons and pumpkins. Broken glass lay in front of unfortunate storefronts that caught stray bullets from the confrontation. Chaos may have been a diluted way to describe the grotesque scene that lay before him. As a couple of men crouched over the dead vigilante, people emerged from makeshift bunkers and barricaded storefronts. The men discovered that their companion had immediately succumbed to his wound, for he lay defunct and motionless on the cobblestones.

Braxton dusted off his trousers and made his way up the street in the direction that the horsemen had fled. He approached where he had tied off his steed to find that, other than a little bit of startling, the horse was fine and most likely as eager to get out of town as Braxton. The two rode out of town and rested at the bridge that overlooked the Node River.

Braxton leaned up against the stone railing that overlooked the churning waters below. The river tore through the grandeur of the countryside with its vicious rapids and carved banks. The Node ran on for miles fueling countless cities that relied on the natural reservoir to provide them with the essence of life, water. Tree branches and other debris floated downstream becoming submerged only to pierce the water's surface moments later. The jagged rocks that outlined the river and sporadically interrupted its flow formed a natural deterrent for curious swimmers and boatmen alike. The waterway was a rose with granite thorns guarding its immaculate waters.

The man collected himself and his thoughts and began the trek back to his cottage on the cliffside. Galileo never seemed to tire under the weight of Braxton, and the two had traveled through countless dales and swamps in every corner of the world. At the end of the day, Galileo would be satisfied to receive a portion of hay and the occasional apple as repayment. Horses are quite simple creatures.

The two arrived as the sun set over the ridge which meant that there were still many hours left for Braxton to prepare for tomorrow. As Galileo meandered through his small pasture, Braxton packed a suitcase full of clothing, basic supplies, and a couple of books. The black leather suitcase was crammed full of stuff that made it seem that Braxton might never return, which was a possible and terrifying reality. Braxton went to his desk which was cluttered with pens, papers, and the glass that had a scotch-colored ring in the bottom from last night's debauchery. The sun set as the man fixed himself a dinner of the remnants of a tin can of cashews, a couple of slices of stale bread with butter, and a hunk of cheese that had somehow not gone bad on the counter.

A full meal was rare in the cottage, for Braxton lived off the land and rarely spent time in town. Most of his sustenance was provided via the cellar that was usually well-stocked from his last venture abroad. The items that lingered in the cellar were always non-perishable and usually kept in casks, waxes, or crates. The cellar had delicacies from all over the world that would make even a well-seasoned chef's palette look like the kid's section of the world's menu.

Braxton continued his packing extravaganza by beginning to load books, suitcases, boxes, and other amenities onto the wagon that would become his lodging for the extent of his travels. The man ended his day with a modest glass of scotch and headed off to sleep.

Braxton awoke to the crow of a rooster, despite not owning a rooster or knowing of one nearby. Glancing out his bedside window, there was no sign of poultry or any abnormality within his yard. After getting ready for what would surely be a long day, he ate breakfast and grabbed the remainder of his valued possessions including his jacket and cap to brave what wonders and horrors lay ahead of him. Leaving the cliffside Shangri La was not the choice many wise men would've made to go seek out some mythological text, but the man who sat in the driver's seat of the wagon was going to do just that. There was no telling when or if the man would return. As the wagon rumbled onto the dusty trail that led towards Blackstone, pans clanged, coins jingled, boxes shuddered, and wheels turned to kick off the expedition that would surely be a stairway to heaven or descent to hell.

The forest and its foliage soon gave way to golden fields of grain that spanned on for infinity, only interrupted by intermittent mills that oversaw the sea of gold. The windmills spun sluggishly in the faint October breeze. The trail ran on through the fields with its sporadic potholes that added only a bit more headache to the journey that was just beginning. Galileo wasn't bothered or fatigued by the burden of the small wagon, yet one couldn't help but pity a creature who worked all day for the highlight to be some dry hay and a morsel of what one may generously call an apple.

The gritty sound of the gravelly trail and the muffled sounds of pots and pans clattering violated the otherwise silent atmosphere of the wagon. Braxton was thankful for something to break the silence because he viewed long periods of it as maddening. A brief spell of silence was a tool for thinking or contemplating, while hours of it can begin to separate one from their sanity. The trail stretched out miles before him seeming as if he had entered a never-ending loop of lush fields and dust. The dust was swept up thick enough in some places to make one believe they had swallowed a sheet of sandpaper if unfortunate enough to breathe in these vexatious particles.

After several miles of coughing, hacking, and other joyful experiences, the form of a far-off city came into view on the horizon. The taste of breakfast had long gone and was now replaced with the taste of dirt and filth that had only been temporarily purged by a few long sips of water from a steel canteen. The mirage of the city came closer as Galileo continued to pace down the strenuous path that had begun to take on a slight incline. A distant train whistle sounded from the depot that sat at the edge of town. Blackstone drew closer as the lettering above the gateway to the town became legible, assuring travelers that this was indeed the Blackstone they were looking for.

The trees flanking the entrance had changed their summer coats of vibrant green for a crisp shade of orange that provided a bit of color to the dull coal mining town. As Braxton's wagon entered the streets of Blackstone, he noticed people coated in coal dust bustling about between carts weighted with lodes of coal and other precious stones. The sound of voices shouting and steel wheels grinding on the gravel streets created a cacophony of what some may call a streetlife serenade. The storefronts in this town were limited to general stores, coal distributor offices, taverns, and inns for the occasional traveler. What more could a desolate coal mining town need?

Amongst the coal dust and pungent smell of livestock and body odor, the day carried on for many who were coming or going to the mines. Braxton picked out the place where he could find Ebner, Samson's General Store. The store was nothing flashy with its peeling gray paint revealing the wooden boards that had seen better days. A minute balcony overlooked the street with an archaic old man sitting and smoking a cigarette that contributed to the already poor air quality. A stairway was fastened to the edge of the building that led up to the balcony. Braxton climbed the rickety stairs to the balcony and noticed that Ebner sat alone, despite there being two chairs on the deck. The man sat silently and solemnly staring out to the life in the streets below and perhaps to the horizon that peeked out from behind the inn's shingled roof across the way.

Ebner Frost sat in his chair smoking his second cigarette of the day overlooking the happenings in the town of Blackstone. The man's routine hadn't changed in twenty years except for his wife no longer joining him. After losing his wife a decade ago, Ebner rarely left his home for the notion that there was nothing more for this timeworn man in this cruel world than the cold embrace of his end. Patiently waiting for what may befall him, the man wasn't dissatisfied or angry with the world, just more or less speculating about his divine fate. Fate was playing the long game with the man, for he often pondered what he was waiting on or if he was simply cursed to remain for eternity as a punishment for a wrong to which he was oblivious. The man was simply just existing. The gusto and energy of a young man had deserted him long ago with the replacement of laze and complacency becoming his new identity. Mining had been the man's life for fifty years before he was able to comfortably retire with his ailing body as his grand prize, creaking and aching joints included. Content to just watch the circus that was on the main street, Ebner waited patiently in his unorthodox waiting room. The monotony of life was rudely interrupted by the presence of a man from afar who had come seeking some sort of holy grail from a man whose purpose in life was to fill ashtrays and mentally remark on the lives of those in Blackstone.

Braxton took in the man with his wrinkled skin, stamped with liver spots, clinging to his bones and the cigarette that spewed smoke into the atmosphere. Braxton kept the poker chip in mind in case this old-timer decided to get confrontational with what little ambition remained in that hoary mind of his. The old man said nothing and gave no inclination that he ever knew Braxton existed next to him. Braxton took it upon himself to break the eerie and awkward silence that hung in the air.

"Good afternoon, sir. You must be Ebner. Pleased to meet you."

The man turned to face Braxton, finally, and used his worn vocal cords to utter one word, "Sit."

Braxton sat in the chair next to the man and awaited a reaction. The grizzled old man set his cigarette into the silver ashtray. Anticipation built between the two as Ebner formulated his profound response, "Why are you here?"

Braxton was puzzled and shocked by the blunt question. The obvious answer was that he was pursuing the *Book of Knowledge*; however, this man seemed to be looking for a more elaborate retort. Explanations ranging from "none of your business" to "this pursuit is all I have" surged through his mind, trying to stifle his desperation and harshness. Like a pill finding its fret on a roulette wheel, an apt response emerged from the mental fog. "I'm here on a journey for something simpler minds cannot possibly fathom, the *Book of Knowledge*."

Ebner raised an eyebrow and gave an unexpected response, "I don't believe this to be so. You are here because you are stranded on

11

a vessel with no captain or crew. You are adrift without a direction or savior in sight. Seeking and losing sight of something are two exceptionally different concepts. You are not here because you require aid. You are here because you are lost."

"While this may be true, this is no mad scramble for some unknown goal. There is indeed a method and a motive for my travels."

The old man considered the reasoning and offered his counter, "Even a blind man wandering in the night is bound to bump into something. Whether or not he finds what he desires is not a question of why but of how. There are no rewards for those who are just well-intentioned and pure, but there is much bounty for those who possess the means to obtain what they long for."

"That's fundamentally why I'm here. Not to become a virtuous saint or dawdle mindlessly but to pursue something that most wouldn't even momentarily consider. I've been told that you could point me in the right direction, so I may draw closer to my objective."

Ebner studied the young man, for he was not sure if the man was a charlatan or genuine in his purpose. Many had tried to obtain the book at one point or another, but none had ever come close. This fact lingered in Ebner's mind. He figured that if the man was who he claimed to be then the book would surely be his; whereas, the man would pay dearly for his lies and deceit if sent further down this dim path. After a deep exhale, Ebner reached his mental verdict and gave the visitor what he wanted. Ebner continued in his worn, stern voice, "The solution to your conundrum exists nowhere and everywhere. I know not of the keeper of this book or its location, but I can assure you it's out there for you. The person who knows most about this talisman would be Asmodeus, a painter who wanders throughout the land seeking his next masterpiece. He's traveled and seen more things than most people in this town have seen cumulatively. He travels in a wagon similar to the one you possess and hasn't been seen in Blackstone for over a year. Many fear he may have perished alongside his artwork. The last I heard of the man was that he was headed towards Hellfire Swamp on his way to Longwood."

Braxton was surprised that the man disclosed such information without further scrutiny or analysis; however, there was a mutual feeling of understanding that dwelled between the pair. Ebner understood two facts of this matter that had influenced his decision: Kingston had already ignited the fire that would either consume or be harnessed by the man now sitting next to him, and there was a spark of confidence that Ebner invested in Braxton. Time would answer all lingering queries that Ebner could not answer at this moment.

The two sat looking at the street life below, watching people walk past carrying beaten pickaxes, toting burlap sacks, and pushing weighty carts piled high with coal. Braxton couldn't believe that the only lead he'd received might be dead or on the other side of this god-forsaken planet. Hope was a fleeting concept that may have sunk to the bottom of the cold waters of Hellfire Swamp alongside Asmodeus's wagon.

As a faint trail of smoke rose from the discarded cigarette in the ashtray, the sun began to set on the village. Ebner and Braxton finally had one final exchange before Braxton's departure. Braxton broke the tranquility after a decent extent of time, "Thank you for both the advice and direction. I should be going now to not waste more of your time."

Ebner kept his gaze on the sunset and replied, "You have wasted no time of mine, for this has been the most use I've had in quite some time. However, do not take what I say in vain. May you stop to take in a few more sunsets on your travels to truly immerse yourself in the journey and enjoy yourself rather than troubling yourself with the comings of tomorrow. I do have one last request for you. Send Kingston my regards and my forgiveness."

After a brief nod of approval, Braxton made his way down from the balcony and walked down the street to a local pub to find food and comfort from the cool autumn air. Pubs, to Braxton, were wells of anarchy, half-witted knowledge, and forgotten sorrows that also provided adequate food to famished travelers. Whether it be considered a haven or hell, Braxton sat at the bar and ordered a modest helping of beef stew. Only a few patrons lined the bar this evening with a couple of unkempt miners and a man in business attire who looked out of place in this rundown town. The bartender was a shorter woman with her auburn hair braided down her back and a pair of warm brown eyes. She seemed to be one of the unfortunate people who got stuck here and could never buy her way out. Braxton's attention shifted straight to the stew when it was set before him.

Food had a peculiar way of eluding the mind until it was set before someone and their barren stomach. Besides not having to cook for himself, the warm stew was a luxury for any traveler who otherwise would be eating out of a dented can or scrounging for the ends of stale bread. To any lord or king, the stew would've been borderline gruel; however, the lack of a complete meal on this day made the stew the equivalent of the finest bisque money could buy.

With an empty bowl and a full stomach, the man finished his drink, paid his tab, and headed back into the night. The shroud of darkness had taken over the street that was now illuminated by street lamps and lanterns that hung from wagons and calloused hands. The night hid all sorts of things, from smuggling operations to promiscuous folks who wandered the walkways. The coal dust hung in the air still now, resembling a swarm of gnats that flocked around the glowing streetlamps. Live insects were becoming a rarity as the fall was soon to turn to winter with freezing temperatures and frost already creeping in. The season of reddened, sniffling noses and dreaded snowfall would surely be upon them soon.

Regardless of the weather, Braxton knew he would continue his journey until he either became literally or figuratively burnt out or achieved his distant goal. The man was not senseless but preferred dedicated and devoted adjectives. In truth, the man knew he had a location without directions, a goal without the means to achieve it, and a mortal body with limits.

Braxton lit the steel lantern that hung in his wagon to provide himself some illumination to get himself situated and prepared for the next leg of the journey. Galileo was harnessed and halfway between indifference and eagerness to break up the monotony of the grimy streets of Blackstone.

As Galileo cantered out of Blackstone followed by the wagon, Braxton sat in the driver's seat and looked up to see Ebner, still sentried upon his balcony above the main street. Ebner had a peculiar way of carrying himself, one that poised itself as perplexing yet reassuring. The man was laced with more knowledge than any library could hope to possess. He knew secrets that would never be uttered and common knowledge that had now been lost to most modern elementary minds. Braxton couldn't decide whether he had

14

made an ally or gained another spectator who awaited developments like a speculator awaiting the winning numbers.

Regardless of what lay behind him, the path before him was set and currently dimly lit by the moonlight that served as the sole guide for Braxton's eyes. Fields stretched to the distant mountains that broke the horizon like spines jutting from the Earth's skin. The night was cool and quiet with the only sounds coming from passing travelers on their warpaths and voyages and from the wheels that grumbled and creaked beneath the wagon. Forward was the only direction that subsisted in Braxton's mind. Here and there, a rustling from the field or a subtle hiss from a garden snake would startle the driver; however, they were brushed off as insignificant nothings of nature. Paranoia and madness were two things that were not needed on this journey yet had somehow crept their way into the wagon with Braxton. Every rustling or part in the grain fields surely was caused by some wild-eyed, rabid beast who would surely be the end of the man and his endeavor. Alas, none of these ghastly creatures came forth from their hideouts and hovels.

The wagon continued on through the winding trails as night set upon the countryside. There were still many miles to be traveled, many deeds to be done, and many people to be seen or found. Despite this daunting feat that would more than likely take a miracle, Braxton was willing to take this voyage one step, or rather, one name at a time. Tired and beaten from today's travels, the wagon was parked beside the road under the shade of sturdy oak. The occupant set himself up a makeshift bed with a stiff pillow and scratchy blanket as his mind slowly was set adrift. There currently loitered one prominent name on Braxton's mind: Asmodeus.

Chapter Three
Hell and High Water

Braxton awoke to the sound of songbirds and the rustling of leaves from the oak above. The lush green grass was primed with its morning dew as the sun began its ascent into the eastern sky. There was a subtle coldness to the air that made one aware that winter was on a collision course with them. While Galileo grazed on the damp grass, Braxton repacked his pillow and blanket back into a crate and went to fetch Galileo from his lawn clipping duties. Once the horse was harnessed and Braxton slipped on his coat, the caravan took off towards Hellfire Swamp.

The aforementioned swamp was not a place of splendor, natural beauty, and pleasantries as the backwaters were littered with thieves, alligators, and other unscrupulous entities. Braxton had ventured to the swamp before but never alone. Most chose to cross the hazardous region with large parties, for there was a definite strength in numbers. At least with others, there was someone to outrun if all else failed.

Rolling golden fields spread for what seemed like an eternity until a dark grove of trees came into view in the distance as the wagon rumbled over a hill. The trees began to draw closer and with it, Braxton began to see a sight that he couldn't have possibly expected. There ran a trail through the heart of the swamp that was frequently traveled. Today, there was no trail anywhere as the entirety of it was submerged beneath murky green waters. What once was the trail was now a boat launch into the filthy water for those who would like to test the buoyancy of their wagons or carts. Braxton saw a wagon beside two men who were sitting atop a fallen log with a map spread between them.

The men looked up from their map and addressed the disgruntled Braxton that had found out the forlorn news they had already discovered. The man who wore a leather tunic spoke up, "Good morning, sir. Hope you don't plan on getting anywhere in a hurry, for it doesn't look like any of us are about to cross this swampland. Someone said the levee broke and the Node River flooded the trails. The only other way around is to go through Hawthorne and cut through some backcountry to get back on the route."

Braxton thought of any routes that may run around the swamp; alas, the men were right. Hawthorne was the best way. The men rolled their map up and put it into a cylindrical holster that was strapped to their wagon. Braxton responded to the man in the tunic, "Well, I'm set for Longwood, so it appears I've got no alternative but to go through Hawthorne and proceed on that path. I appreciate the advice gentlemen, and who might I owe my thanks to?"

The two looked at each other and then the man with the haggard beard spoke, "I'm Theo and he is Lac. We are men who've been sent out to intercept a traveler by the name of Braxton Sterns by the order of the crest. You wouldn't happen to be he?"

Braxton looked the men over and noticed that they both possessed swords in sheaths at their belts and each had a patch on their tunics that held the crest of Lord Drummond, a prominent figure who owned thousands of acres near Hawthorne. A response brewed in Braxton's mind, preferably one that wouldn't get a sword lodged in his ribs. These two men were hopefully not Drummond's finest. By the route the men had instructed him to take, he would pass right by the manor where the cowardly lord resided.

The two armed men looked inquisitively at Braxton, but the pair didn't seem to know of the ruse quite yet that was being perpetrated before their enervated eyes.

A simple response was all Braxton uttered before taking off down the trail, "Thanks again."

There was an exchange of glances and shrugs between the two baffled sentries. Braxton made his way towards Hawthorne along the detour that would surely add a little more excitement to this journey. Planning was suspended for the time being with the only objective remaining to pass through Hawthorne and reach Longwood alive. Unfortunately, Braxton hypothesized that Lord Drummond would do everything in his malevolent power to hinder his efforts at living.

Braxton and Lord Drummond had a long history of disputes, dealings, and deceits with most of the negative aspects being contributed by his lordship. Fault only lied with Braxton on one offense where he had revoked his promise to supply Drummond with information regarding a merchant who Drummond would have most likely killed and pillaged wares from due to the merchant not paying a hefty tax to him. The merchant repaid Braxton with the stock that now lay in the cellar of his home, unknown to Drummond. A pitstop at Drummond Manor was not on the itinerary, but it could certainly be squeezed in now.

Following a brief ride full of vengeful thoughts and tranquil countryside, Hawthorne came into view. Hawthorne was a bland town with its cookie-cutter storefronts and uniform rooflines and streets. The place looked like the architect had the creativity of a box of saltines for nothing spoke of any sort of character or awe with its elements of wrought iron and brick.

After passing through the desolate streets of Hawthorne, the countryside resumed with cornfields replacing the fields of grain he had become fond of. The corn had long lost its moisture and assumed a dull yellow hue as it awaited honed scythes and leathery hands to cut it down. Braxton's wagon occasionally would pass by a wagon or travelers who would pay no mind to the stranger as they were assuredly on their path to their destiny or demise. A couple of these passersby wore a similar patch to the one donned by Theo and Lac which made Braxton slightly perturbed.

These thoughts of suspicion and angst soon vacated his cerebrum as he focused on the endless fields that bordered the trail. Just as he grew accustomed to the orderly expanses of maize, the Drummond Manor came into view looming over the field like a tenebrous colossus observing its crops. Just as every dog must have his day and every drunk must have his drink, every conceited lord must have his pompous estate in the middle of nowhere. As the features of the mansion came closer, one could pick out the bold brickwork, marble masonry, and trimmed topiaries that reassured the beholder that this place belonged to someone with as much pride as wealth. Something wasn't quite right though, for few people were moving about aside from a gardener trimming a hedge and a man stoically standing guard by the entrance. Crimson curtains covered the front windows. Braxton parked his wagon under a stout hickory and tethered Galileo to the trunk, so he could devour as much finely-manicured grass as his ravenous gut desired. Walking up the gravel driveway, Braxton scoured his mind for a reason that the Drummond estate could look so lifeless. The guard stood stiffly by the doors and fixed his gaze on the approaching traveler.

Garrison North had been working for Lord Drummond for five years as a sentry and secretary of sorts. The man stood guard outside the doors of the manor during the afternoon hours taking messages and dismissing lousy beggars. Today was no different, aside from a man who seemed to take immense interest in the recent news that Garrison had conveyed. The news had not impacted Garrison much at all for the only changes that were implemented were a new face to answer to and a new signature on payment forms.

Braxton approached the man at the door in a cordial manner to hopefully answer the questions that roamed his mind. Vengeful and snide comments fled from his mind to be replaced with those of curiosity and intrigue.

The guard greeted Braxton before he could even think of much else, "Good day, sir. What business do you have here?"

Braxton evaluated his questioner and concisely responded, "I've come to seek counsel with Lord Drummond the First."

"Not today or tomorrow or the next day you won't. Lord Drummond is dead. Succeeded only by his son, Lord Cardoff Drummond. Unless you wish to settle something with Lord Drummond's heir, I suggest you save yourself the time." The guard motioned towards the way Braxton came.

Without another word, Braxton sauntered away from the door towards the road with thoughts of pity for an old companion clashing with a distaste for an old adversary in his mind. There was no importance in how or when the man had died, for there simply was one grim conclusion to reach. Jameson Drummond was dead.

Friend or foe, there was a familiarity with Jameson that obligated Braxton to feel sympathy and grief for the loss. Beyond forged bonds and vindictive pettiness, we are all human at the end of the day.

Braxton harnessed Galileo and the two set off down the trail once more. The fields resumed as wheels creaked and thoughts crept into Braxton's mind. Crossroads appeared in the near distance, indicating the route he had taken had circumvented the flooded swampland. As the wagon turned onto the new road, Braxton picked out a couple of crows that were pecking at a pair of dilapidated ears of corn. The crows seemed indifferent towards the traveler for their attention remained affixed to their bounty. Miles of dirt and dust awaited before the wagon would arrive in Longwood.

The corn eventually gave way to pasture where wooly sheep preyed on the viridescent grass below their hooves. Poorly maintained fences lined the fields with some consisting of rotting boards and rusted nails. Despite this flaw, the sheep sought no necessity to exploit this weakness, for they possessed all the luxuries that a barnyard animal could ask for.

Braxton continued to sightsee and admire the sheep with their lush coats and scenic pastures. An understanding of a shepherd's contentment with this kind of life began to formulate within Braxton. The only disruption in the landscape came in the form of the crumbling ruins of a stone cathedral that now had a sycamore tree sprouting from the center of its hall. The few pews that remained were either smashed or tipped over. Devout worshippers had deserted this place long ago, yet it still stood as a hallowed shadow of its former glory. The only attendees to the site now were sheep and sorry shepherds who needed shelter from the occasional rainfall or raging wind. Galileo seemed to be amused by the sheep and vice versa, for the two parties seemed to eye each other in passing.

Continuing further down the trail, the air became slightly more comforting as the parky autumn air reached its afternoon high temperature. Comfort had been an afterthought on this journey; however, nature seemed to be compensating aptly for his poor planning. There was one persistent goal on his mind and the cold and grief would not be near enough for him to even consider scrapping it. Asmodeus was still out there and hopefully breathing. This was far from over, and the worst was yet to come.

Chapter Four
A Painter's Perspective

The trail ran on for what seemed like forever. The fence lines and pastures continued with their sheer vastness reaching out for the horizon. While Braxton attempted to remain awake holding the reins, Galileo trotted towards Longwood. Longwood was a peaceful town where chalets and boutiques were bunched together to form a makeshift series of streets and allies. As the caravan neared the town, smoke crept into the air from the stone chimneys that clung to the side of the cottages. After hours of wheels churning and dust inhalation, Braxton and Galileo had reached Longwood. The next step would be to find the needle in the haystack.

Sprightly storefronts lined the streets with display cases exhibiting cakes, clocks, shofars, and countless other trinkets and goods. The clocks pilfered Braxton's attention with their intricate carvings and functions such as a whimsical cuckoo bird that would sporadically pop out of a small door. The smell of wood varnish and autumn leaves made for a euphoric scent that almost had an intoxicating effect on the mind. Then again, it may have just been the chemicals from the varnish. Braxton soon dismissed his fascination and continued down the lane to find two people he had not seen in quite some time, his parents.

Patrick and Leona Sterns sat on their front porch in their respective rocking chairs. The pair had been married for thirty years, and the rest was history. Neither of them had any complaints or discontentment with their situation as they had both retired last year to pursue a life of comfort and ease in their humble abode. Patrick smoked his corn cob pipe while Leona worked on crocheting a scarf for the upcoming winter months. An old newspaper sat on a small table next to Patrick, who had heard all the news he could handle for the day. Patrick was a workaholic who had reluctantly retired from clock-making at his dear wife's request. He had worked to earn everything he possessed in life and had few besides himself to thank for his assets. Leona had worked as a seamstress for a local tailor named J.R. Schmidt for decades. Patrick and Leona had both found their callings and then subsequently retired from these positions after copious years of hard work and dedication to their crafts. They both mutually agreed that they had hoped their son would do the same. This was not so.

As the wagon rumbled down a familiar street, Braxton prepared himself for what was about to occur. He couldn't predict whether it would be another nuclear fallout or a heartwarming reunion. His childhood home came into view, bordered by the Jones's and the MacArthur's who had been neighbors for what seemed like forever. On the front porch, his parents sat doing everything and nothing simultaneously. Smoke from his father's pipe streamed upward into the rafters while the clicking of needles indicated that his mother was not quite fully retired. As the wagon came to a stop in front of the house, Braxton's mother looked up from her project.

Leona bolted to embrace her estranged son who had chosen to visit them for once. Patrick shifted in his chair to gaze upon a man he almost could not recognize after all these years.

Braxton was glad to see his parents; however, he wondered just how glad they were to see him. His mother nearly tackled him while his father sat in judgment, still clutching his pipe firmly between his lips. Approval was a touchy subject around his father, but Braxton had grown to seek approval only from himself and any other party his actions may directly concern. Despite these notions, the bond between the two was undeniable despite the bit of alienation time had driven between them. For his mother, she had always been the kindest and gentlest soul to walk the earth. She was one of the few who Braxton could always rely upon for support no matter what crazed passion he pursued. His father was not of the same sort.

Patrick set down his pipe and focused his gaze on Braxton who was now bound tightly by his mother's clutch. Times had changed with Patrick. He had grown to accept that Braxton was who he was and that was all there was to the matter. No amount of derision or scorn would take away what the boy possessed. Mr. Sterns was still torn on whether to respect Braxton for his independent spirit or to fear for the path his open mind would set him on. Making a brief and hasty choice, he decided to trust Braxton with his own fate. With his doubts aside, he stood to greet his son.

Braxton could begin to feel his father's cold presence despite the warm embrace of his mother. However, there seemed to be a fondness that had sprung up in his dad. The eyes he now looked into weren't filled with criticism or unsolicited advice, but rather they were filled with acceptance and respect. Braxton briefly glanced upward to ensure that the sky was not about to fall and crush this reunion. The clouds still hung in their place.

Braxton was bombarded with questions and concerns from his mother while his father approached the pair. A side effect of being as compassionate and caring as his mother existed in constant worry and speculation about the well-being of her little boy, who was currently thirty years old. His mom wiped grit and dirt from his face with her polka-dotted handkerchief and sputtered sweet nothings through her tears. After his mother collected herself and Braxton greeted his father, the trio migrated inside to chat and grab something to eat. Mrs. Sterns prepared a tray of small sandwiches and a pitcher of water to set on the table. Not much had changed within the kitchen, for the same outdated kitchen chairs loitered under the same glass light fixture that had furnished the home since his boyhood. Looking into the modest living room, an old portrait of his parents hung on the wall above the mantle that depicted his mom and dad stiffly standing next to one another. That was probably the longest the pair had stood still in quite some time. The portrait was no longer accurate for his father's jet-black hair had now turned gray and his mother had acquired faint dark circles beneath her once flawless emerald eyes. He'd like to think his parents aged like fine wine as opposed to spoiling like moldy cheese.

Braxton sat across from his father as his mother set the tray and pitcher in the center of the square table. His mother took the chair between the two like a mediator overseeing negotiations to cease the war. Despite these past tensions, the pair were not at each other's throats nor did either bother to make subtle jabs. Braxton's father asked him about the usual parental subjects of his finances, his interests, and lastly, his job.

His finances were fine seeing as he still had a home to return to and his interests were scattered but enough to keep him occupied. On the other hand, employment was a sensitive matter, as Braxton had never been a conventional company employee or tradesman. The man preferred to travel and make his hay by trading goods and acquiring foreign wares to bring home. These wares ranged from paintings to wood carvings that littered Braxton's cottage in a fashion that some would call disorderly hoarding. Braxton viewed himself as an unwonted merchant while his father viewed him as a haywire drifter who needed to learn a useful craft.

Braxton evaded the subject by careening the conversation towards his parents and the handful of happenings of Longwood and their daily lives. Not much of interest ever happened in Longwood with the highlight of some weeks being the grass growing another inch beneath everyone's feet. His parents viewed it as pleasant and amply satisfying to live their lives in this place. This was an unfathomable possibility for Braxton.

As the ice cubes melted in the pitcher and sandwiches slowly disappeared, talk of the neighbor's new grandson and the recent weather nearly made Braxton ready for a lengthy nap. One detail of the conversation; however, caught Braxton's attention. The rumor of a strange man wandering on the outskirts of town.

Braxton dug deeper into the subject until his father told him that one of the neighbors claimed to have discovered the man's tent and wagon strewn about near Sutter's Hill on the edge of town. Sutter's Hill was the site of a famous battle centuries ago, but now it served as a scenic spot for a picnic or a viable hill to send a sled down in the winter. Apparently, the place was now fit to be the campsite of an abstract painter.

The conversation began to dissipate as the afternoon trudged on. The minimal news his parents could share burnt out and small talk eventually became repetitive and boring. Around two o'clock, Braxton bade farewell to his parents with one final hug from his mother and a firm handshake from his father. As his mother waved him goodbye from the porch, the wagon's wheels began to turn again. There was a new destination, Sutter's Hill.

The streets of Longwood were nothing of excitement with the occasional passersby going about their day or the sporadic creaking of a hanging sign. Barrels, boxes, and bins were being moved about outside a warehouse while a group of songbirds sat on the eave of the building chirping away. A pair of men in overalls and leather boots stood against the side of the building talking about their families and lunches. The taller of the two apparently wasn't fond of his wife's cooking.

As the wagon left town, Sutter's Hill came into view. A sturdy oak had sat atop the hill since Braxton's childhood and still remained. However, the tent, wagon, and easel that sat beneath its branches were additions recently made by quite the eccentric man.

Asmodeus Grimes stood at his easel overlooking the town of Longwood. In one hand, he held a paintbrush that would paint his next masterpiece. In the other hand, he held a briar pipe that would surely shorten his career. He gazed at the cityscape and began painting the start of the building. The man's convoluted mind raced with brilliant and mad ideas that he would translate into brush strokes and paint blotches in due time. His left hand ached under the bloody bandage that sheltered his fresh wound from the elements. At his age, his once-dark beard had begun to welcome new shades of grey and white to the unkempt mess. To Asmodeus, life was in a constant state of organized chaos that some would refer to as reckless, yet he could find comfort in the unpredictability and surprises of tomorrow. He knew not where he would be next week or the one after that; however, he was sure he would find his way. The sun began to descend from the sky.

Braxton and Galileo beheld the encampment from afar. There was a white tent that was nestled under a tree while a man stood at an easel overlooking the town that sat in the valley. A wagon was present with its steed napping beneath the branches of the oak. A vacant spit sat unmoving above an extinguished fire that was nothing more than a pile of smoldering ash now. Braxton's attention shifted back to the man who stood with his back to him. The only choice that was evident was to approach the strange man and pray that the man was not psychotic or deranged. He wasn't completely unstable.

Braxton approached the encampment and called out to the man, "You there! Are you the painter, Asmodeus?"

Asmodeus pivoted to face the source of this disturbance and uttered from his crooked mouth, "I am he. Have you come to kill me or rid me of what few valuables I have left? If so, help yourself."

Slightly bothered and a little confused, Braxton assured the man he was not there to shake him down for his gold or other riches. He was there to talk. "I've come not for your materialistic belongings, but rather for some information I believe you possess. If you would so have me I would be greatly indebted to your hospitality."

The painter evaluated this response and humored the oncoming visitor, "This much is satisfactory, but I can't promise that I'm any well of knowledge. This well has long run dry much as the desert sands."

After taking care of Galileo, Braxton sat on a wooden crate near the painter. continued to collect colors from his palette and smear them on the canvas. An image of the city below began to develop on the canvas as the man continued his work. Braxton didn't want to interrupt the man's process yet he had to find what he was looking for. The gauze-wrapped hand bothered Braxton, for he wondered how such an injury had transpired. He figured it would be better not to inquire. One shouldn't mess about if one isn't prepared to find out.

Braxton opted to ask about what the man knew of the *Book of Knowledge*. "What knowledge might you have of a text by the title of the *Book of Knowledge*?"

The brush strokes ceased as Asmodeus contemplated what this stranger might want with such a talisman. "You do not want this item. The book possesses qualities that no man is fit to handle unless he seeks his undoing. The achievement of obtaining this particular text would prevent you from accomplishing much else on this mortal plain. If you find this book then you might as well arrange to be buried with it."

While this description worried and perplexed Braxton, he was not sure how much to trust a man in the position of Asmodeus. For all he knew, Asmodeus was playing games to try to source a chuckle at Braxton's expense. The man seemed direly serious in his words though.

As the painting progressed where the whole city could be identified, Braxton responded, "Well, if I wanted to find this cursed relic then where might I find it?"

Asmodeus continued his painting and answered, "If you must pursue your demise then you may want to ask yourself why. I will offer you what you desire, but first, you must be self-assured it is, indeed, what you want."

Braxton pondered for a minute as to why he wanted this book. He was certain he had a valid reason but couldn't seem to locate it. Was this blind confidence or merely a gut instinct that he was following to the end? He recomposed himself and decided that he was still hell-bent on finding the book. "I'm quite certain that the book is what I want, now where might I find it?"

Asmodeus assessed the confidence of the man and concluded that his ambition would lead him towards it one way or another. The man was already in freefall so it couldn't be unwise to make his landing a little more bearable. After all, everything that goes up, must come down, especially hope. He gave the man what he wanted, "You'll want to find an alchemist by the name of Merlin. He lives in an abandoned mill on the outskirts of Merchant's Grove. Anything I know of this book I've heard from him."

The city has been painted and Asmodeus's brush moved to the sky. He dipped his brush in a glob of crimson paint that had been slightly mixed with black. The resulting sky that was painted looked like a churning, hellish mass of dark swirls in a blood-red sky. Hell seemed to have leaked into the heavens. Braxton did not comment on this aspect of the piece. The pair continued to chat until the afternoon turned to night. Asmodeus leaned the painting against the trunk of the tree and lit a quaint fire from what little firewood he had left. Shadows of the two men flickered across the wagon behind them. The pair ate and drank deep into the night until only crickets and moths stirred about the hilltop. The conversation between the two frequently changed from stories of their youth to recent adventures through picturesque dells and colossal ranges. Asmodeus shared one of his philosophies with Braxton. "Just because we wander does not mean we are lost vagrants without purpose. We simply just haven't found our groove in this vast world."

This struck a chord with Braxton that not much had ever been able to do. Some folks could just never comprehend what would possess another to never settle down, and that was fine. Those who needed to know knew. Braxton sipped more spring water from his canteen as Asmodeus scooped beans from a dented tin can. The pair truly weren't so different after all.

As the night aged, the two turned into their wagons after extinguishing the fire and checking in on their horses. The night was quiet aside from the chirp of a lonesome cricket and the faint snoring coming from Asmodeus's wagon. A shrill breeze blew through the wagon as Braxton drifted off to sleep.

When Braxton awoke, he was alone with his wagon and Galileo. The painter was gone and all he had left was the painting that still leaned against the tree trunk. Braxton prayed that the painting wasn't some cryptic harbinger of tragedy to come, but it was rather some dismal musing conjured up by the artist. Braxton stowed the painting in his wagon and began to clean up the aftermath from last night which consisted of a blanket and an empty canteen. For some peculiar reason, he felt like he was being observed from far away.

The painting haunted the man's mind, yet he cast it aside as pure premonition and fantasy. Braxton got his possessions packed away and his mind in order. Merchant's Grove was quite far, but at this point, there was no sense in even contemplating conceding. He doubted that Merlin would be the man to simply hand over the book, yet optimism wasn't completely lost. Wagon wheels began to churn and dust kicked up as the caravan took off for its next expedition down the trail.

Before he could reach Merchant's Grove, Braxton would have to make a pitstop in Asheville. Asheville was a port town that Braxton frequented as he sourced his favorite scotch from a distiller by the name of Wesson. The city wasn't much to look at if you weren't looking to buy overpriced spirits or drink your sorrows away. The fields of grain reappeared as Braxton distanced himself from Longwood, and the next destination was far from the only thought weighing down his mind at the moment. Windmills turned and the wheat fields waved to and fro like an unruly ocean. Braxton saw a scarecrow amongst the crops and wondered what such an existence of simplicity would be like in a raggedy pair of overalls and a sun-baked straw hat. One could only hope that a few pesky crows would be the biggest disturbance in their life. With the reins in one hand, Braxton took bites out of an apple that would serve as his breakfast. As his stomach growled, he would give anything for one of his mother's homemade muffins or his dad's fried eggs. Times like these remind us that we are truly alive.

Chapter Five
The Harboring of Thoughts and Ships

The smell of seawater and hops filled the air along with the clinking of chains and shouting of boisterous sailors. Asheville was in full swing with barrels rolling and taps spewing the nectar that millions adored. Masts, with gulls resting on them, could be made out above the warehouses and breweries that people migrated between. Braxton was not here to procure his favorite spirit, but he was rather here to rest himself and restock his barren wagon and gut for the miles ahead. The afternoon had just arrived with many weary sailors and energetic tourists seeking refuge in the nearest pub. Lunch didn't sound half bad to the man and his void of a stomach that hadn't eaten a proper meal in quite some time. A strong porter and a well-seasoned filet of salmon didn't sound too off-putting to the traveler. A chalkboard sign out front of Stark's Pub advertised a salmon special and local brews which were all the convincing Braxton needed. Gulls cawed and door hinges squeaked as Braxton walked into Stark's.

The sounds of a piano hung in the air amongst the cigarette smoke while people indulged in conversation, drinks, and food. Braxton found himself a stool at the end of the bar and ordered himself a drink and a lunch special. A pianist sat on a wooden piano bench and smoked a cigarette while he meticulously and masterfully caressed the keys before him. The music pierced through the murmurs of the establishment and seemed to keep all of the patrons content. A trio of familiar eyes sat at the bar's other end with bandanas around their necks. The one who sat closest to Braxton had a handlebar mustache and a crooked grin pasted onto his face. The middle one sat and fiddled with a matchbox that sat on the counter while his companions sat and jabbered about pointless topics. The third sat the farthest away with a scar across his left eye and his bulky figure leaning on the counter. An empty ashtray sat in front of the men as well as a couple of gold coins that glimmered on the bar's polished surface. Evidently, the men found pleasure in stealing riches from others rather than stealing years away from themselves with a pack of smokes. The man that sat nearest to them looked to be weeping with an assortment of empty glasses in front of him. He had certainly found a way to drown his woes in booze momentarily. When he sobered up, his tab would certainly not bring a smile back to his colorless face. The parallels of a pub were fascinating where you could have a lively celebration next to a man who appears lifeless and pale from hardships suffered.

A warm plate of baked salmon with chips was placed before Braxton who had now found his own distraction from the world. The food soon disappeared as did the cold glass of porter that now only served as a vessel for a few droplets of condensation disrupted by the man's finger markings. The plate was cleared aside from a few resilient crumbs and specks of what the man hoped was food. After his plate's departure and appetite's quenching, he paid his tab and headed outside into the cool afternoon that had draped over the town.

Braxton decided to walk out to the harbor to take in the grand ships and the ocean. He found a spot on the end of a short pier that was worn and battered from years of water slapping its surface and the sun beating down on it. A nearby ship had an intricate crest of some lord from a far-off land printed on its sails with the name of the mighty watercraft painted in gold lettering on the hull, *The Golden Asp*. This feat of naval ingenuity sat in the harbor with its towering masts and polished silver cannons. The boat bobbed up and down in the active waters while men loaded barrels and boxes over the starboard side of the railing. Braxton gazed to his left and picked out a small fishing boat that was tethered to the otherwise vacant dock. That small ship had sailed to countless harbors and docks in its life, more than most could ever dream of seeing. Whoever the captain of that vessel was had surely seen foreign shores and remote islands that would never be beheld by any other pair of eyes. Braxton had traveled near and far, yet he still had miles to go. Knowing these things could make one feel small.

Buoys rested on the water's surface as bells rang out on *The Golden Asp*, indicating that it was time to depart. Men in tricorn hats scrambled for their positions as one man untied the rope that anchored the ship to the sturdy dock. After a while, the ship that had once dwarfed Braxton was a minuscule speck on the horizon.

Braxton got up from his viewing spot and dusted off his trousers. As he turned to walk back up the dock, he noticed the flit of a curtain in a second-story window that aroused suspicion in the man. An urge drew Braxton to investigate the residence from which the oddity had been spotted. He knocked on the front door of the building and waited for a couple of minutes. At last, an old man leaning on a cane slowly opened the door much to Braxton's confusion. Was this old codger some sort of creep or just a curious dweller of the quiet town?

Braxton warmly greeted the man, "Good afternoon, sir. How might I find you this fine day?"

The old man furrowed one of his bushy brows and replied, "I'm just fine, thank you. What business do you have with me? I don't want no pamphlets or divine advice."

"My apologies for the intrusion, but I have a small question for you. Who lives on the second story of this residence?"

"No one to my knowledge, it's just storage that's connected to my residence on this floor. Why might you ask?"

"I saw something strange on that floor through one of your windows. Would you mind if I investigate this anomaly?"

The old man looked Braxton up and down with a puzzled look. He finally responded, "I don't mind, but all you'll find is some dust and some old relics."

The old man and Braxton walked through the man's living room and walked up the stairs. A door with a brass doorknob barred the pair from the storage area. Opening the door revealed much of what the old man had depicted, a dusty grandfather clock, a few empty frames, a small chest of keepsakes, and an old dresser that was missing a couple of handles. One aspect stood out to the pair: one of the windows was open that led onto a neighboring rooftop. The blue curtains on the ajar window swayed in the wind as Braxton looked to the old man who was already en route to close the drafty window. The old man commented, "Well, that's a bit odd. A hinge or something must have rusted and allowed that to swing open. I appreciate your watchful eyes, young man."

Braxton said nothing, but he knew something was off aside from a pair of rusty hinges. This old man didn't seem privy to the presence of whoever was just in his attic, but Braxton had no intentions of unnerving the old man with something that could just be considered some manic conspiracy.

The pair walked downstairs, and Braxton bade the man farewell and thanked him for his hospitality. As Braxton walked down the street, he tried to put the puzzle pieces together to form a picture, yet he seemed to be missing something. He couldn't quite figure out what it might be.

While he walked past lit warehouse windows that displayed stout copper stills inside, a crisp breeze blew down the cobblestone streets that were devoid of life aside from a flock of gulls and a small group of tourists. Autumn leaves littered the streets from the trees that loomed at the end of the lane. The pounding of metal could be heard from a nearby blacksmith shop that had a burly, dark-haired man hunched over an anvil with a hefty hammer. Braxton walked to the outskirts of town where he found his wagon and Galileo waiting patiently. After the wagon was set to proceed its crawl through the countryside, Braxton got back into the driver seat and gently cracked the reins.

The sites of Asheville faded into a distant blur while the caravan made its way toward Merchant's Grove. A fog began to settle upon the countryside as Braxton passed fields that were now devoid of their crops as the harvest had begun. Carts passed by heaped with corn, wheat, and barley stacked high and haphazardly. Men in straw hats and blue overalls tended to these wagons as they made their way toward Asheville where they would be generously rewarded for their wares. Other passersby included wealthy merchants, with their silken robes and well-stocked carriages, and wagons with empty kegs and barrels that had some urgent business in Asheville. Braxton chose to enjoy the countryside, unlike these tunnel-visioned, money-seeking folks who had committed themselves to their lives of competitive pricing and underhanded dealing. An old farmhouse sat in the distance on a hill that overlooked the barren fields and the men who toiled to scrounge up the remainder of what was left. Braxton was trying to do the same with himself. He aspired to put together the scraps and fragments to make something that would resemble his true self.

Braxton hoped that this book could give him a sense of where to start; however, he had begun to collect more questions than answers on this lengthy endeavor. The man was left with questions without answers and answers that truly didn't fulfill the queries that burned into his brain. There had to be something more.

Hope existed on some distant horizon, and it was merely a matter of learning to obtain this sacred commodity. The course was set for Braxton, yet he felt that there was more to this charade than just a man chasing after a fabled book. He was determined to climb to the highest peaks and stoop to the lowest canyons to find what he was looking for. No matter what tragedy or temporary bliss this world allotted him, he would brave the tempest to grasp what he longed for. The wagon's wheels continued to roll, and Galileo trotted onward.

Night began to settle on the man as the bustling town of Merchant's Grove came into view. Merchant's Grove was a particularly unusual town where rather than being made up of the haves and the have-nots, there existed the classes of the haves and wannabe haves. The distinction between the two groups was difficult to discern, but there were small signs, much as a shaky hand at the poker table or a brief grimace at the price of a finely tailored suit. The place crawled with debtors and debt collectors who made their living off of one another. There existed an equilibrium where the debtors must borrow to live and the rich must loan money to become more affluent. To exist in this environment was pain, yet a fine bottle of champagne or an expensive cigar could help most take the edge off. If the streets were lined in gold then it was a debtor's weepings that kept them shining and immaculate. Braxton had to find a man who was attempting what everyone else in this amoral town was attempting, turning nothing into gold.

Chapter Six
Not All That Glistens is Gold

Radiant chandeliers and candelabrums lit up the residences and storefronts that bordered the street. Like moths to these flames, nightlife proceeded between different restaurants, pubs, and shops with men in well-fitted suits and women wearing elegant dresses. Then there was Braxton in his shabby attire of a white button-up and black slacks. This town could make the middle class feel like a pauper while making the rich seem like common folk. Wealth flowed through the streets like an autumn breeze as a parade of fine silk and polished canes proceeded down the main street. The scent of expensive cologne and foreign perfumes lingered in the air like a mist, distorting what lay beneath these heavenly aromas. Bankers, loan sharks, gamblers, and businessmen flooded the streets with their heartless forms wrapped in expensive cloth and secured with rings and watches of precious metal.

There was a range of ages on the street, from young investors who looked like they just barely had leaped into their twenties to ancient men who Braxton presumed were bankers and loan sharks as it was certain that the evil would live forever. Old men were prevalent everywhere with their leathery, wrinkled faces sporting a constant sneer. It would seem that money does not buy you happiness, but rather an everlasting sense of shrewdness and bitterness.

Proceeding down the crowded street, Braxton felt isolated from the snobbish mass that emitted sounds of important conversations and a stiff atmosphere that made the world almost seem still amidst the dull glamor. Doorbells chimed and voices chattered as the crowd slowly crawled down the street. Golden and silver accents lined the sides of the cement-and-mortar storefronts that advertised everything a wealthy nobleman could need, from overpriced fragrances to flashy rings and watches. Amongst these alluring shops, debt collector offices reminded everyone of the price of their purchases with a few sheepish faces ducking into these establishments from time to time. As the town square drew near, Braxton could make out the smiling bronze head of Pierce Wallace, a beloved philanthropist and businessman, looming over the bustling streets. Every person on this street strived to be like Pierce; however, most of these wishful thinkers didn't possess the morals or ethics to be in the same league as him. Pierce was the acting mayor of the town who had more money than anyone could possibly care to spend. Despite his status, he chose to live modestly and donate a good sum of money to charitable foundations and the city to keep the world around him turning. Anytime that Pierce chose to give a speech or address, the square would be crammed with every crumby investor and sly salesman that the town could offer to listen to Pierce's insightful words. Many of his principles and ideas were cast aside by his listeners who had quotas to meet and wares to peddle to plentiful wallets. Morals and profit margins can scarcely coexist.

On this dreary autumn evening, there were no speeches or philosophies to behold. A light rain dampened the streets and the exquisite attires of socialites who scattered for cover due to their lacking of an umbrella. The cold droplets of rain were refreshing bullets that washed away the dust from Braxton's face and clothing, but the rainfall posed one problem. Braxton was now cold and wet with a slight shiver running up and down his spine. He sought shelter in the Gilded Eagle Inn which lay at the end of the block.

The inn had a few guests in its lobby, wrangling luggage and drying off. A clock on the wall behind the front desk read eight o'clock as the innkeeper leaned temperamentally on the counter. Braxton got himself a room and headed upstairs with a room key and suitcase in his hands. His new dwelling overlooked the square with the friendly left eye of Pierce staring right at his window. The rain pattered on the window pane as Braxton looked out into the night sky to observe the plentiful constellations that studded the dark expanse. After the stars could offer no more of their wonder, Braxton changed his clothing and retreated to the bed in which he plunged into sleep amidst the cotton sheets and feather-filled pillows.

When he awoke, the sun glared through the window to blind the groggy traveler. After this inconvenience, he got up to collect himself and set out to find Merlin. Braxton had no idea what to expect of Merlin, but he hoped that his little endeavor would come to a brief close soon. He laced up his boots, straightened his collar, and headed for the door. After returning his key and exiting the Gilded Eagle, he made way for the other side of town to hopefully find out where this elusive informant lived.

The streets this morning were deserted compared to last night with only a handful of vendors and tourists roaming about the streets. Braxton believed that he would be able to find out where Merlin lived by finding a local farmer who had surely explored the nearby countryside and perhaps encountered the alchemist. People dressed in overalls and jeans were hard to find in this pretentious town where such lowly beings never desired to tarry. After much searching, Braxton found a man sitting on a wooden crate outside a small restaurant that exuded the smell of black coffee from a nearby open window. The man had a long coppery beard and one of the buttons on his button-up shirt was missing. He sat whittling a small sculpture of an owl out of a chunk of wood. It reminded him of the friendly creature that had perched itself in his modest cottage's rafters several days ago. Braxton greeted the man, "Good morning, sir. I couldn't help but notice the fine little masterpiece you have there. Would you be interested in selling it?"

The farmer pocketed his knife and looked up from his project to assess the man before him. He felt that the stranger was almost as out of place as himself, so he felt inclined to engage with the outlier. "Morning, I may be, but I don't want your money. All I request is you humor me for a bit and this little piece is yours."

Braxton sat on a nearby box and responded, "I'd be delighted to as long as you'll have me. How might the harvest have gone for you this year?"

"The harvest was swell with a hearty yield as well as high prices. There's a shortage across the bay apparently so all those middlemen in Asheville paid tenfold what they would've in a normal year for my grain. Now let me pose a question. Why is a man such as yourself in a town like this?"

"Well, I'm here to talk to a man named Merlin who lives near town. You wouldn't happen to know where this man resides?"

"I don't know much about the old coot, and I haven't the slightest idea what you might want from him. He lives about a mile north of here."

"Well, I've been told the man has something I want."

"What might you want from the man? A dose of insanity? A vial of snake oil? Or maybe you'd prefer a profound nothing? In any case, you might wanna steer clear of that mess."

"I don't have much of a choice in this matter, but I appreciate the warning."

"If you must, then do as you will. However, I must thank you for your time and the brief entertainment you have provided me, much like this small project here."

Braxton tucked the owl into his baggage and left the man to his own devices. He was now disturbed and intrigued by the warning, for it seemed oddly similar to how people described Asmodeus. Maybe people aren't always what everyone paints them out to be, and we just merely need to find our opinions for ourselves rather than borrowing someone else's.

Braxton returned to the stable where he had stored his wagon and Galileo as the morning crept towards the afternoon. He gave the horse one of the last apples that remained and stowed his luggage back in the covered wagon. After hasty preparation, Braxton and Galileo set out to meet the alleged mad scientist that inhabited a run-down mill.

The countryside was a breath of fresh air for Braxton who was thankful to be free from the urban bonds of the city. Empty fields and farmsteads lined the road as Braxton headed in the direction that the farmer had told him. After half an hour, a spire came into view on the horizon that looked quite suitable for a deranged scholar. Tattered blades struggled to spin on the exterior of the structure as the caravan inched closer.

Merlin Drachman stood leaning over his latest experiment as the afternoon hour approached. Beakers bubbled and vials fizzed as Merlin scampered between stations, wrote notes, and made adjustments to his convoluted systems. Hours, days, and months had been devoted to this attempt at finally creating the Philosopher's Stone and proving the world wrong. Everything was going according to plan until a tube exploded, spewing blue liquid across the entire table and onto Merlin's white shirt. The man cursed at his damned luck, but he was snapped out of his fit of rage by something unusual. There was a faint rapping at his door.

He used a stray rag to clean up his mess and wipe down his shirt before heading downstairs to greet this untimely visitor. The last time the man opened the door it had been a missionary trying to convert the countryside to some new revolutionary faith. This time it was quite different.

Braxton stood awkwardly at the door, awaiting an internal response from inside the mill. Just as he went to walk away, the door creaked open to reveal what most would've called astounding. This did not look like a man who could perform the groundbreaking feat of turning anything into gold. The man before him had bushy eyebrows and a white beard that nearly ran down to his beltline and a shirt stained with something blue that Braxton didn't dare ask about. The strangest detail, however, was that the man wore nothing more than a shirt and a pair of red polka-dotted white boxers. Shock was an understatement.

Merlin broke the uncomfortable silence with his usual friendly greeting, "What do you want?"

Braxton averted his gaze back to the man's aged face and managed a quick response, "Are you Merlin?"

"Depends on who you ask, but I do believe that's my name. Can I help you?"

"I've been told you know something about the *Book of Knowledge*."

The old man eyeballed the young man before him prior to answering. "What could you possibly want with such an item? It doesn't have much of a resale value you know."

"Well, I believe it might contain some information that I might require."

"If you're looking for information, go stick your nose in an encyclopedia instead of my business. Whatever information you seek is not worth the price you'll pay."

"So, you do know about this book?"

"Of course I do. I'm the last person to ever lay eyes on the text before it was sealed away by the Knights of Dark."

Braxton's eyebrows sprung to life. Who were the Knights of Dark and what did they have to do with the book? His curiosity got the best of him and he inquired further. "Who are the Knights of Dark and how are they related to this book?"

"You better come inside before I tell you that."

Braxton followed the man inside the mill to a sparsely furnished living room that was occupied by two stiff red chairs and a small coffee table that had books and empty mugs littered on it. The walls of this place were lined with crowded bookshelves and scientific instruments that Braxton was clueless about. After drawing the downstairs curtains over all the exterior windows, Merlin finally put on some moderately clean pants and a red robe and returned downstairs to sit opposite Braxton.

Merlin adjusted himself in his chair and took a sip from a ceramic mug that had a little steam coming from it. "So what do you want to know?"

"Anything you're willing to give to aid me in my endeavor, for I am in no position to make demands."

"Well, at least you have that understanding. What I am about to tell you is something I've kept to myself for quite some time. I'm reluctant to tell even you, but I shall not live forever and I'd rather put the book in your hands rather than the corrupt hands of those who are also pursuing what you seek. The Dark Knights are an ancient group of people who assembled the *Book of Knowledge* through methods now lost to the modern-day mind. Stories of people of yore claiming to have seen some enchanted text have all come into contact with this talisman, but few have recognized what their eyes have seen. This book has influenced countless civilizations, religions, and cultures that may never know where their ancestors gained their knowledge from. Many people were tied to this work from the brightest of minds to the wealthiest of lords. Most of the creators and their heirs are now long gone aside from a few who may never be heard from again due to their preference for solitude. The last heir I heard of was a lord by the name of Lord Drummond from over by Hawthorne, but I haven't the faintest idea of who that man was. I seem to be one of the last heirs left, yet you are the first to have consulted me on this topic. The only information that remains of the book in my possession would be the location of the Keeper."

The old man paused to nervously glance at a nearby window and take a sip from his mug. Braxton felt as if he had just earned himself a new burden as well as a new journey to embark on. The man continued again, "The Keeper lives in the logging town of Ramstead, but the rest of the information is not as convenient as what you're probably hoping. I wouldn't recommend you disclose this riddle I'm about to share, as it could be lethal if the wrong someone figures out what you're after: 'An Archer of the Heaven's nemesis possesses hope for the mindful traveler.' That is all I was left, but I am in no health to be going on any expeditions. The Keeper should be able to answer as to where the book now lies, but I make no promises. If I could offer you more assistance I would, but I fear anything else I can tell you would be irrelevant or more harm than good."

Braxton produced a small journal from his pocket and jotted down the riddle that would mock him and halt his progress until it was cracked. After returning the journal to its pocket, Braxton made one final remark to the old man, "I cannot thank you enough for your advice and trust, but I fear the game has only begun. Lord Drummond is dead and I fear I'm in more peril than I've realized. If I find this book, I promise you'll be the first to know. You may not realize what you have done for me, but your wisdom is worth its weight in gold."

After bidding the alchemist farewell, Braxton and Galileo proceeded out into the golden sunlight and toward the horizon to travel to Ramstead.

Chapter Seven
A Sign of Hope

Ramstead was eons away, yet Braxton felt content to coast through the evergreen forests and mountains. Rolling brooks provided the man with fresh water as well as a bit of serenity to ease his hyperactive mind. The trail became ridden with pine needles and cones as the foliage became more clustered. Galileo seemed to enjoy the scenery with his endless hoof clops being the only disruption to the sounds of the earth. Braxton would occasionally pull out his journal and read the lines to himself, but he couldn't seem to find an answer to this vexatious riddle. He also pondered who else may want the Book of Knowledge for themselves and where they might be. The man felt as if he knew everything yet also nothing at the same time, but it was more than likely his paranoia plaguing his mind.

The wagon creaked and groaned as it endured the rough trail that ran through a pass in the Sawridge mountains. Sawmills and logging camps dotted the hills amongst the stout pines that awaited the first snowfall of the season with outstretched arms. Scents of pine and fresh mountain air made the man breathe a bit easier and helped to calm his troubled nerves. A striking elk stood in a clearing, munching on the remaining green grass that littered the ground. With its massive antlers, the beast had eluded hunters for quite some time. Braxton couldn't help but feel that he too was being hunted. Squirrels rustled in the trees as the wagon passed beneath their lofty branches while an industrious woodpecker bore into a distant tree.

Braxton stopped momentarily to gather a few huckleberries from a nearby bush as the forest went about its day. After donating a few of the berries to Galileo, the ride continued, and the afternoon sky began to fade. The man had only seen one other wagon all day that was hauling lumber with a man in a red-plaid shirt sitting in the driver's seat. Night fell as Braxton lit a lantern and continued his journey toward Ramstead. Stars littered the sky as the crescent moon showed through the sparse clouds. The evening air grew cold, and the woodlands grew silent as the birds retreated to their nests and the squirrels to their knot holes. A twig snapping to the right of the trail alarmed Braxton whose mind was still polluted by paranoia. Towering pines swayed in the nightly winds that sent a chill through Braxton.

After an hour, the lights of a small settlement came into view. The homes were all log cabins with splintering and worn-out sidings that had seen their fair share of weathering. A lone inn stood out above the cabins with its second story looming above the surrounding squat homes. Braxton decided he would spend the night in the shelter of his covered wagon which was beginning to become futile against the icy air. For the first time since this journey began, Braxton felt that he could use a glass of scotch. As he sat with his glass, he examined the riddle that burdened the page of his journal. He thought back to his childhood of stories told by his father who had a knack for creating the most interesting fables. Braxton was not the most attentive in his younger years and scantily picked up much from his father's nightly tales. However, many of his father's stories pertained to the constellations that now hung in the night sky. Braxton realized something.

What if all this time he had known the answer? What if this solution laid right above his head, before his very eyes?

In his homesickness, Braxton had found his answer. The story of Orion and Sagittarius came to the forefront of the weary man's head. Sagittarius had been an archer. Orion had perished at the hand of some entity, and Sagittarius had vowed to avenge the man's death by killing the creature. Actually, Orion had not perished by the hand of anything, but rather, he died by the stinger of a scorpion. This was the answer, a scorpion. So why was he in the middle of the woods looking for this mythological arachnid's relation to his predicament? There had to be more to this than just an ancient story and a bunch of stars, but maybe it was truly just that. Simplicity has a deceptive element about it that makes it almost complex.

While this excitement began to cease, Braxton was now faced with a new question: what did the people of Ramstead know of scorpions? Braxton decided that this query would have to wait to the morrow for an answer as his body needed some rest.

With the arrival of a new day, Braxton packed away his glass and blanket. He rubbed his eyes and began to walk towards the town. As he walked into the inn, the innkeeper looked up from his newspaper and greeted the newcomer. The smell of musty wallpaper and burnt wax hung in the air as the candle on a nearby table burned what little was left of its wick. Braxton responded to the man politely, "What might you know of any scorpions around here, sir?"

The man issued a perplexed expression and then responded, "Nothing more than a desert dweller knows of a snow blizzard, why might you ask?"

"Well, I was given some directions and all I can remember of them is the word scorpion. Are you sure there is nothing of the nature or name here in Ramstead?"

"Now that you mention it, I do believe I heard someone's earlier rambling about something that might be related. He went on and on about some gypsy he ran into when hiking up in the mountains a couple of miles east of here. The man said the gypsy was at an overlook called Scorpion's peak or something like that. I quit eavesdropping after that, for I don't concern myself with aimless wanderers or their lunacies. I hope that helps for what it's worth."

"Thank you for your time, sir."

With that notion, Braxton exited through the creaky inn door and was greeted once more by the cold embrace of nature. He knew his destination, yet several questions still required answers and many problems still remained without solutions. Homesickness still troubled the man who longed for something more familiar and fond than the same old trail he had grown accustomed to. Despite Braxton's longings, the wagon proceeded down the trail back towards the Sawridge mountains to find another foreign face.

The evergreens shivered in the cool breeze as the wagon rumbled down the dirt path. After half an hour, the man picked out a grouping of tents and wagons that seemed to be some sort of logging camp that was on its way out of the wilderness. The sound of wood being split by sharp axes and rowdy voices pierced through the tranquil forest, reassuring the assumption that this settlement was definitely a logging camp. As he neared the encampment, a surplus of beards, flannels, and hatchets caught his eye amongst the band of bulky lumberjacks. A few of them shot unfriendly glares and curious glances towards Braxton and Galileo but most continued to chatter and sip from their tin mugs. Braxton stopped his wagon and picked out one of the more friendly-looking lumberjacks who didn't seem to want to flay him with the head of their axe.

The couple of bearded men that Braxton approached turned to face him. He was greeted by the taller of the pair, "Are you lost there, sir? You don't look like much of a logger to me."

"Well, not exactly, but I could use some directions if you would. Would either of you gentlemen know how to get to Scorpion's Peak?"

The shorter of the two looked up at the other and then provided an answer, "I believe it's a mile east of here up on Miller's Trail. Might wanna steer clear of that area for there's rumored to be a few black bears roaming those hills. You wouldn't happen to have any booze on your wagon, would ya? We've been running a bit shallow lately."

Braxton decided to repay these men for their directions. He rummaged through his wagon until he found something, a sealed bottle of whiskey from over a year ago. As he didn't care much for the spirit, he gifted it to the men to hopefully make their logging venture a bit more bearable. What he didn't expect was for one of the men to return the favor. The taller of the men unfastened his hatchet from his belt and placed it into Braxton's empty hands. The wooden hilt was smooth and polished with a gleaming head that seemingly could penetrate the densest of oaks and pines. Braxton thanked the man and exchanged a few more words before his departure. After his barter with the alpine loggers, the trail resumed with its winding paths that led to higher altitudes and thinner air.

Braxton remained observant for any black bears or other predators who wouldn't be as hospitable as the group of unshaven lumberjacks. The occasional crash of a falling pine deep in the forest signified that the lumberjacks had achieved another success that would certainly be celebrated by another round of indulgence and banter. As the lumber camps and swinging of axes became a faraway memory, Braxton came across a wooden post that had various arrows pointing in different directions. Each of the arrows read off a different trail name but Braxton only cared for one: Miller's Trail.

After lacing up his boots and tethering Galileo to a nearby tree, Braxton set out on the narrow trail to meet with fate.

Chapter Eight
Insightful Visions of the Blind

Braxton walked for what seemed minutes short of an eternity, but at last, the man reached what he hoped was the peak. As he approached the area, he heard the chords of a guitar streaming down the hill and through the pines. When he finally reached the peak, he stared into the back of a man with an acoustic guitar laid across his lap with a fire burning bright in front of him. The odd man sat on a small crate and didn't seem to pay much mind to the approaching hiker. A faint humming could be heard from the seated guitarist as he strummed his instrument. Braxton paused for a moment a few paces away from the man to analyze his situation, and he came to the realization that he wasn't going to meet too many ordinary folks on this journey. A bit peculiar was an understatement for this individual.

Braxton interrupted the man's harmonious tune with a brief greeting, "Good evening, sir. You wouldn't happen to be the man who is known as the Keeper, would you?"

"Well, Braxton. If you must know, I go by many names, and the Keeper is one of the lot. I was hoping you would show up soon, as it's getting a bit cold out and this fire can only keep one warm for so long."

Braxton walked before the man to establish eye contact, but he was appalled to see that the man's eyes possessed no pupils, and he seemed to be blindly playing his guitar. Braxton asked the obvious question, "Are you blind, sir?"

"We are both blind, but not in the same way, my boy. My physical condition doesn't allow me to behold the green grasses or the blue skies, but I am not sightless. I understand what I am and what exists around and before me in my life, but your uncertainty and indecisiveness have crippled your sight much worse than this cruel form could ever hinder mine. You possess the ability to limit yourself and set yourself free, but you still clutch the key firmly in your tired fingers."

"While you may have a point, that's exactly why my weary self stands before you in these worn-out boots and this sweat-ridden shirt. I'm certainly not here because I possess all the answers or virtues there are to have. We all walk this earth blindly, but it is the times in which we catch electrifying glimpses of the true nature of ourselves and the world around us that truly define who we are. I've come to you in hopes that you'll open my eyes a bit more and offer me a minuscule piece of insight into the *Book of Knowledge*."

"What I can offer you will only be minuscule in hindsight, but I must tell you that you are about to cross a threshold through which you may not return. Grave dangers await all those who pursue the *Book of Knowledge*, and I cannot promise you anything."

Braxton noticed something strange about his situation. Firstly, he referred to Braxton by his name without any introductions. Secondly, the burnt end of a cigar sat near the edge of the blaze of the fire. The Keeper had put all his cards on the table finally and so had someone else. Braxton decided to test his hunch with the blind fellow, "You wouldn't happen to have a spare cigarette or cigar on you, would you?"

The Keeper shifted on his crate and replied, "Absolutely not, I've already lost my sight, and I don't aspire to do any more harm to this dilapidated form of mine."

This raised some eyebrows for Braxton as he had more than likely found a piece to this puzzle. Kingston Devalve had been here. Braxton was not quite sure for what or why, but that con artist had stood on this peak and more than likely had spoken to the Keeper. The possibility that Kingston was out exploring nature when he wasn't stealing money from amateur card players and happened to bump into the Keeper seemed to be a bit too good to be true. A flood of questions and suspicions surged through Braxton's mind as he formulated his next question for the Keeper. The sky began to darken as dawn started to set upon the overlook. Braxton broke the brief silence, "Have you spoken to anyone recently about the *Book of Knowledge*, besides me?"

"Well, as a matter of fact, I did a day or two ago. A poorly mannered fellow who seemed very dead set on prying everything I know of the talisman. That man is about to wander into a trap from which he won't return. I sent him on a perilous route through Foster's Woods, a grove occupied by a psychotic slaughterer who will make quick work of the men."

"Wait, there was someone else with the man?"

"I believe so even though the second man didn't speak much. The one man referred to his companion by the name of Mr. Freeman, if I remember things correctly. Anyway, I have no tricks or gimmicks for you since you've been much more entertaining and cordial than that last nuisance. To unlock the book's vault in Wanderer's Keep, you'll need to get five shards of a medallion referred to as the Knight's Crest. The first piece resides in a bookshop outside Shephard's Pass by Havenstein. You'll have to talk to the librarian, Heidi, to find out how to get it though."

Braxton began to ponder his options as the Keeper fell silent. He wanted to help Sean, but there was no guarantee that the pair were not already strung up from the highest tree in the forest. If he didn't try to save Sean, the thought would haunt his mind for eternity with what-ifs and pangs of guilt. However, he wouldn't have much to think about if he went after the endangered party and ended up joining them in the madman's grasp. The choice hung in the air like a guillotine blade awaiting the man's fateful verdict. In the end, Braxton mustered an ounce of compassion and concern and decided to try to save his friend from a forest-dwelling nutcase. However, Braxton had a couple of other questions for the Keeper and his seemingly all-knowing mind.

"Do you know where Wanderer's Keep is or where to find out who or what does?"

"I can't look you in the eye and say I can, but this endeavor will surely unveil the location from its shroud of anonymity. I wish you the best of luck on this journey, for you are about to become a contender in a game that seldom few are knowledgeable of and most wouldn't even think to undertake."

"Is there any other assistance you are willing to grant me before I depart?"

"As a matter of fact, I do have one more thing for you that I'd like you to deliver. Do not lose it and do not even think about opening it." The blind man reached out his hand and offered a white envelope with a red seal on it to the traveler. "This item is intended for a man I haven't seen in quite some time, a man by the name of Ebner Frost.

He's an older fellow in Blackstone who will immediately know what is in the parcel if you mention me. By the way, it seems I've failed to introduce myself properly. I'm Horace Walker, and who may I owe my thanks to?"

"Braxton Sterns, sir. However, what you have given me is all the thanks I require, and as for what you have requested, I will see that it is done. If we have nothing else to exchange, I should be going now for the night and we are not growing any younger. Thank you, Horace."

With that, Braxton began to walk down the slender trail back towards Galileo and the wagon. Stars began to dot the sky as a faint guitar could be heard in the distance. Horace had opened Braxton's eyes to his own fallacies and follies while also granting him intel on his next destination, Foster's Grove. For a blind man, Horace had a knack for observing the small matters and putting them together to form a larger puzzle that many were oblivious to. Braxton tucked the envelope into his jacket pocket as he descended from the hillside. The packet felt light as a feather with its contents more than likely a piece of parchment. A temptation to open the envelope didn't exist within the man who figured the letter would mean much more to the intended recipient than the prying eyes of the messenger. Some things are best left unopened and unknown.

The fact that Braxton would get to see a familiar face was a welcome surprise for a man who was learning just how small a world it was in which he roamed. He couldn't decide whether or not this repetitive trend was a curse or a blessing in this carousel of names and faces. Familiarity was something that Braxton could use a bit more in the arduous travels that had taken him over every hill and under every bridge these lands could possibly provide. As the guitar's melody faded into nothing, Braxton was engulfed in the serenity of the pines. The trees rustled in the wind as the temperature continued to creep into colder depths. As he exited the trail, his attention shifted to Galileo who had found shelter under the arms of a gargantuan pine. Galileo stood with a brief neigh as Braxton worked on harnessing him back to the wagon's chassis. The pair soon disappeared from the site and traveled through a pass in the mountains. Foster's Grove was on the way to Havenstein, so maybe Horace had not completely misled the men. Braxton had heard stirrings of Foster and his antics, but he had never paid much attention to the subject. He'd once heard that the man was a practitioner of witchcraft while another rumor had alleged that the man was just not quite right between the ears. These accusations were taken with a grain of salt for one may not look into fanciful gossip and obscure details, distorted at a mind's leisure, too far.

The mountains soon loitered quite some distance from the wagon as the agrarian countryside that was now a flat expanse of torn-up farmland. The fields that had once been decorated with golden waves of grain now sat vacant with nothing but the dull hue of brown crop soil as a reminder of the once grand scenery.

The wind began to dissipate as the temperature had acquired a noticeable chill that wasn't friendly to wandering men or horses. Every breath that Braxton and Galileo took was now visible as vapor in the cold air. Braxton began buttoning his coat as Galileo proceeded forward down the trail that was certainly frozen beneath the steed's hooves. Attempting to eat a piece of cold bread, Braxton's arm trembled from the cold that had disregarded his sleeves as a minor obstacle. The lantern that hung from the side of the wagon failed to provide any warm comfort aside from its glow that lit the path ahead.

Rummaging through his clothing, he found a wool scarf and a pair of gloves to cover his shivering fingers. Braxton was elated to see a quaint inn in the distance with other wagons parked nearby. The Rambler's Inn wasn't much to behold, but it was a tropical paradise compared to the bitter tundra that awaited one outside. Settling into his room, Braxton began to feel his toes once again and changed into his nightly robes. The man gazed out the window into the inky abyss of the polar night. As he gazed out the window, he was appalled to see something he had not seen since last May. Small snowflakes had begun to descend from the heavens. Winter had arrived.

Chapter Nine
Debts Paid and Parcels Delivered

As the sun appeared over the horizon, Braxton awoke and rubbed his groggy eyes. The man hastily packed his few belongings back into his suitcase and bundled up in a jacket and a plaid scarf. He zipped his suitcase and headed downstairs and went out the door, into the stiff morning air. A thin blanket of white coated the vacant fields that surrounded the inn for miles, but it gradually grew thicker as snowflakes gingerly continued to fall.

Braxton fetched Galileo and the wagon from the stable and began the next leg of the journey down the snow-covered trail. Galileo's hooves no longer thumped against the hard ground, but rather, they lightly crunched in the fresh snow. There was about another mile to go to reach Foster's Grove, but the stretch seemed like it would take a millennium to cover. Despite his brief bout of pessimism, the grove soon appeared before him. A stone cottage sat in the middle with its window illuminated and its poorly-kept straw roof. Smoke billowed from the thin chimney that ran up the side of the abode, meaning Foster had a fire burning in his hearth to cook what could presumably be the madman's breakfast. Braxton's attention was caught by a nearby wagon that was parked under a tree without any occupants. Hopefully, the vehicle had not been the hearse that brought Sean and Kingston to their graves. After parking his wagon far from the cottage, Braxton crept closer through the snow to gather his surroundings and determine what fate had befallen Sean and Kingston. Braxton peered through a frosty window to see Foster sitting in an old rocking chair in front of the fire brandishing a cleaver. There was a beaten rug on the floor beneath the chair and the floorboards looked to be heavily worn.

Foster Seward sat in his rocking chair, admiring the flames that danced in his hearth. He had finished polishing his cleaver and had sat down to make himself a pot of oatmeal over his fire. He had caught two trespassers yesterday and had swiftly dealt with the threat by locking the pair of hostile wanderers in his cellar. Foster was pleased to have some company, but the presence of others would be short-lived as he had larger plans for the two. His maddened mind ran wild with grotesque ideas, as well as the longing for some hot oatmeal. He slightly giggled to himself as he thought of how foolish the men had been to bring themselves to his doorstep. As he ran his hand through his stringy hair, Foster thought he heard something from outside in the snow.

Braxton had found the entrance to a small locked cellar and used his hatchet to pierce through the rusted chains that secured the door. This had created much more noise than he had anticipated, so the man had to move quickly to open the cellar doors. The scene in the cellar was not a glamorous one as he saw Sean sitting on the ground near a smashed crate while Kingston sat in the corner on a stool next to what looked like a human femur. The pair beamed when they saw Braxton, but Kingston seemed to be assessing how to take advantage of his savior rather than thinking of how to flee the lair of the madman. Sean got to his feet and attempted to dust off his filthy attire without much result. There was a hole in the cellar ceiling that allowed one to see into the quaint cottage and the smell of something comforting wafted through the opening. *Was that psychopath making oatmeal?* Braxton thought to himself.

The oatmeal became irrelevant when the three men looked up to the top of the cellar steps to see Foster standing there, cleaver in hand. Kingston and Sean looked at each other as Braxton pulled the hatchet from his belt again. Foster shouted down the stairs, "Who goes there?! You will pay dearly for this intrusion!"

The smell of smoke caught Braxton's attention. Braxton looked up to see that the fire no longer remained in the hearth and that it seemed that the rug above them had caught fire from a stray spark. Foster seemed unaware of the flaming rug, but everyone else was certainly aware. Foster had now descended the stairs and stood eye to eye with Braxton. The madman's fingers quivered with the cleaver in their shaky grasp. Braxton had no time to negotiate with the man before Foster lunged forward. It was over in an instant. Foster crumpled to the ground with the hatchet blade protruding from the side of his torso. The maniac writhed and screeched as blood seeped from his wound. Kingston took this time to attempt an escape. However, he was not quite successful. Foster grabbed Kingston's leg and pulled him to the ground.

Kingston yelped as he fell to the floor. Foster used his final moments to purge the world of one more gambler. With his last burst of adrenaline, Foster drove the cleaver into the chest of Kingston. After a few seconds, both men lay lifeless on the ground with blood smeared across their faces and clothing. Sean and Braxton were speechless. Kingston's and Foster's breathing ceased.

Braxton and Sean fled the scene as the whole cottage had become engulfed in flames. It was safe to say that there was no oatmeal to be had. The pair of survivors retreated back to Braxton's wagon to find Galileo had taken notice of the fire. Sean broke the shock-induced silence, "What the hell was that? Why are you here?"

"I heard that Kingston had double-crossed me and had led you both into danger. He wanted to pursue the Book of Knowledge for himself. Now I've got a question for you. Why are you here?"

Sean looked a bit more sheepish now that he had questions to answer, "Well, it's a long story. Can we at least get away from here? I'll explain once we find someplace that isn't near a burning madhouse?"

"Fine, but you've got a lot of blanks to fill in."

The pair rode off in the wagon towards Blackstone as Sean began his muddled explanation of how he ended up entrapped in a madman's cellar in the middle of the woods. "I got myself into this when business wasn't going well last year. I nearly had to sell my pub, but I was offered a lucrative alternative by Kingston. I signed a lengthy contract that I half-read and paid royally for my catastrophic lapse in judgment. Kingston ended up taking advantage of me and putting me in more debt than I started. He kept my pub afloat as long as he could run his poker ring in the back and under the stipulation that I kept the taps running to make him more money. Kingston offered to relieve me of my debts and give me the pub back if I helped him find this book you two are after. I am dearly sorry for getting you into this mess of a charade."

"Well, consider your debt paid because that account just burned up it seems. I understood you had some financial troubles, but I had no idea you were this tied up in debt. On the bright side, all your obligations are fulfilled and Kingston no longer has you under his thumb."

"Yea, I suppose, but I feel we both have a long road ahead of us."

The road, or at least the trail, was a long one to Blackstone. Galileo seemed unfazed by the newly acquired passenger, but the creature didn't seem quite fond of the snow on his metal horseshoes. Frost had begun to form in Sean's orange beard which only seemed to make the poor man shiver more vigorously. Sean's skin had become as white as the snow around it, aside from his cheeks which glowed red under the cover of his facial hair. Snowfall had halted, yet frigid winds still tore across the vacant fields and occasional hillside like daggers of ice looking for skin and cloth to pierce. The two made attempts at conversation on the ride, yet silence was common between the pair of mentally-reeling survivors. After many hours of teeth chattering and comments about the unbearable cold, the dreary town of Blackstone came into view in all its dull splendor. The town was now more colorless with the grass being coated with snow and the trees devoid of any leaves which made one almost feel they were looking through a black-and-white lens. The coal that had once been piled in carts in the streets was now being put to good use in every household's furnace and stove. Gray smoke filled the air to the point where the sun was a faint blur in the clouds of dust and pollution. Braxton broke the silence between the two, "We'll have to stop here for the night as I've got some business to attend to in town here. You're welcome to seek refuge in a pub or an inn, and we'll reconvene in the inn. I'll have us back in Havenstein by the late afternoon tomorrow, but for now, you should go find a warm place to relax and have a bite to eat with this here."

Braxton dropped a couple of coins into Sean's palm. Sean was not one to argue, so he headed for the nearest pub with a working furnace and hot food. After letting Sean off, the wagon proceeded down the street to a familiar general store. As Braxton drew near, he thought it odd yet sensible that Ebner was not perched on his usual chair on the raised balcony. Braxton climbed the rickety stairs and knocked on the door to no answer. All the lights inside the apartment were off which gave Braxton an uneasy feeling. He decided it would be best to see if Samson had heard anything of the old geezer from upstairs.

Samson looked up from his notepad as the door to his store cheerfully chimed. A man in a black coat entered with his face flushed of pigment and plastered with a look between concern and curiosity. Samson greeted the woeful stranger, "What can I do ya for, sir?"

"I'm just curious about the resident who lives above this establishment. Is he out of town?"

"Well, he lived above this establishment. The sorry fellow passed on about five days ago. They managed to bury him outside of town in the cemetery on Godric's Hill before the ground completely froze over. I'm sorry if this is the first you are hearing of this."

"You have nothing to apologize for. Thank you."

With his grim discovery in tow, Braxton somberly walked out of the store and into the deserted street. Braxton knew where he had to go.

After a brief walk to the cemetery, Braxton entered through a wrought iron gate that creaked as it was pushed open. Flanking the pillars that held the gate, stone gargoyles oversaw the coming and going of mourners, gravediggers, and priests. Some who came to the place were not lucky enough to leave and ended up six feet under the topsoil. Braxton immediately picked out a small gravestone that had signs of overturned dirt near it. The tombstone depicted the full name of Ebner, Ebner Williams Frost, and the dates by which the man had lived and died. Braxton almost shed a tear through the blistering cold, but he thought that Ebner would not have wanted the man to waste such a precious commodity on him. Braxton produced the note from his coat and set it against the tombstone that shielded the paper from the wind. Braxton hoped Ebner would receive the correspondence from Horace in due time. A crow cawed in the near distance as Braxton said a brief prayer and walked out of the cemetery.

If all the world a stage, then life is the biggest tragedy to be performed on its hallowed surface.

Chapter Ten
The Keeping of Books and Knowledge

Weighted with his sorrow and grief, Braxton walked back to town to find a place to find something to eat, for he had eaten nothing since that morning. As the sky darkened, street lamps came to life, and Braxton entered a familiar pub. The same auburn-haired bartender stood behind the counter with the usually wistful look on her face that soon turned to a customer service smile as she offered Braxton a drink. It seemed that not everyone could leave this town as Ebner Frost had managed.

With her ball and chain of bills that needed paying and money that needed earning, the waitress got Braxton a beer and went back to polishing the bar counter with a tattered rag. After a few sips from his draft, Braxton troubled the young lady for a plate of food to which she was happily obliged. The man ate and drank his fill and left the pub which had begun to be filled with boisterous and rowdy patrons who had sampled the tap a few too many times. The night was quiet with the only sound being the faint rumble of voices from the pub and the sounds of someone beating a rug down the street. Braxton took himself to the Blackstone Inn and got himself a room. As he walked down the hall, his attention was caught by what he thought was Sean slipping into a room with his arm around a woman.

Braxton minded himself and entered his own room to settle in for the night. Gazing out a second-story window, Braxton observed the streets that Ebner had once surveyed to find that everything was still, aside from a wagon slowly making its way down the main street. When this bit of excitement was stifled after a short time, Braxton changed his clothes and headed off to sleep.

When he awoke, Braxton got dressed for the day in a simple pair of black jeans and a white button-down. As he put on his black leather loafers, the sounds of footsteps down the hall made his ears perk up. He opened the door to find Sean heading down the stairs to the lobby with a key in his hand. Braxton entered the lobby as Sean was speaking energetically with the man behind the counter whose name was apparently Cedrick. Sean seemed to be giving his condolences to the young man for some reason. Braxton decided to find out why.

"Hey Sean, how are we this fine morning?"

Sean turned to face Braxton, "Not too bad, I was just catching up with Cedrick here. Are you about ready to depart?"

"Getting there, but I don't think I've ever formally met Cedrick." Braxton turned to look at Cedrick.

Cedrick chimed in, "I don't think we have. You've probably met my dad though, for that man knew everyone. I'm Ebner's son."

Braxton couldn't believe this. He managed to formulate more conversation, "Well, I heard the news. I knew your father a bit, and I'm sincerely sorry for your loss."

Braxton shook Cedrick's hand as Cedrick began telling the tale of how he and Sean had met when they had both been younger. Cedrick looked young for his thirties with his boyish face and fair skin, but the most defining feature of the man was that he looked distinctly like his father minus the wrinkles and thinning hair. As Sean and Braxton gave their keys and final condolences to the chap, Cedrick remembered something. Cedrick's last visit with his father had been a day before his death, which granted the man some closure and one other thing he intended to give to someone else. Rummaging through the contents of a drawer, Cedrick pulled out a silver pocket watch and handed it to Braxton.

"Here, my father wanted me to give this to you. He said that it would have some significance to you," Cedrick explained.

"This timepiece has some significance to me indeed, thank you."

With the watch now tucked into the pocket in which the letter once rested, Braxton exited the establishment followed by Sean. Braxton knew the message that Ebner was attempting to convey from beyond the grave, but he had no idea how long or how short of a path he had to follow yet. The man was on the clock, literally and figuratively, for there were other men with prying eyes and grimy hands seeking out the *Book of Knowledge* for their own conceited and callous reasons. While Braxton's motivations weren't exactly saintly or selfless, he at least wasn't going to auction off the book to the highest bidder or exploit the text for its darker knowledge. There was no desire to live a life of caviar and cigars or any inclination that the man might be some power-hungry wannabe tyrant. The man simply wanted to know one thing and one thing only: *Was there something more for the man in this broad expanse?*

As the men rode out of Blackstone, the morning sky remained cloudy and glum with its swirled mass of dull grays and mute silvers. The road and its surroundings were just as bleak with the snowfall blanketing every square inch all the way to the horizon. Sean attempted to get water out of a mostly frozen canteen as Braxton guided the wagon toward the bustling streets of Havenstein. After crossing the familiar stone bridge that arches over the Node River, Havenstein came into sight with its cobblestone streets and hanging signs that hung defiantly against the winds. Soon, the hanging sign and storefront that was Freeman's pub appeared. After a brief farewell to his old friend, Braxton continued on his path to the bookshop that sat on the outside of town. The man had passed by the place hundreds of times on his travels, yet he never stopped to investigate the ordinary place. As he entered the business, the bell cheerfully chimed and the woman at the front counter pushed her glasses up her nose and looked up. Her golden crescent-moon earrings swayed as her head tipped up.

The lady greeted Braxton in a warm and friendly tone that was smooth like honey, "Good morning, sir. Is there something I can help you with today?"

Braxton returned the gesture, "Same to you. You wouldn't happen to be Heidi would you?"

"Depends who's asking, but for now I'll entertain this. Yes, I would happen to be her I believe."

"I was sent by a man named Horace Walker who told me you could help me with something."

Heidi looked annoyed as she brushed back her frizzy black hair out of her eyes. "I think I know where you're going with this, and my uncle really needs to give me a heads-up if he's going to start sending more of you travelers my way."

"Wait, Horace is your uncle? Small world I suppose."

"Indeed, he is and you're not wrong. I suppose you are looking for a shard of the Knight's Crest, and for some cosmic reason, it's my responsibility to help you find it. In that case, follow me."

The lady stood, and as her shoes clacked against the hardwood flooring, Braxton couldn't tell if she was annoyed with Horace or him. Heidi showed the man to a small space in the back that had a small table with a chess board laid into it. Both sides were set with medieval characters ready for a mental battle. Braxton didn't understand though. It wasn't as simple as beating Heidi in chess to get the shard, was it?

Heidi began to explain, "Sit. In order to get the fragment, you'll have to win a game of chess, and no, it isn't against me for I haven't the slightest clue on how to play. The board will move along with you as you play and make its own moves to attempt to best you. I can't offer you anything more than that. Good luck."

With her instructions given, Heidi walked back towards the front to resume her position behind the front desk to peruse papers or stamp books, whatever it is that librarians do. Braxton sat at the empty table with the white pieces on his side and the black facing him. The man hadn't played chess in over a year, but he felt he could dust off his rusty skills. He made his move and awaited a rebuttal from the other side. The same piece that Braxton moved assumed an identical position on the other side of the board. Braxton had a hunch as to the gimmick of this paradox. He continued to make moves as his invisible opponent continued to counter with the exact same move set. The board just reflected whatever moves Braxton made. What a novelty. In order to best this entity, he'd have to outsmart himself. He scratched his head as he tested the water by taking a pawn from his opponent. As expected, the black side mimicked the same action. Braxton supposed that he wouldn't be able to simply outmaneuver the entity by utilizing his advantage of moves.

The game went on until something odd happened. He found himself in checkmate as his opponent had made its first original move to exploit a vulnerability in his offense. He had somehow lost to himself. The board reset and all the pieces stood stoically in their places, ready for another onslaught. After hours of gambits and tactics, Braxton had lost countless matches and gained nothing aside from frustration and a developing migraine.

Braxton knew there had to be a way to best the perplexing game, yet he couldn't quite decipher what that revelation was. Whatever possessed these pieces to move was miming his actions until it became beneficial to take a new route, so one had to predict their own downfall prior to it occurring. Maybe that was the trick. The player goes on believing that they have it all in hand until they eventually find out there is always an improved method to their obsolete tactics. It was truly quite humbling, and quite aggravating.

As the morning turned to afternoon and the afternoon careened towards the evening, Braxton finally came to a favorable position where any weakness that showed in his line was reflected across from him. However, there was one fallacy in Braxton's plan that was also now evident in his opponent's. Braxton made the first offensive move and took a leading pawn from the front lines of his opponent. After the pieces were laid down and all moves were made, Braxton had gained his first advantage of the day. All that was left was for his opponent to move his Queen and the game would be finished. He had done what he had once thought impossible. Instead of some complex and intricate scheme, he utilized the simple strategy of striking before he could be exploited through a brash offensive rampage through his opponent's line. He had run the table on himself. As his opponent's queen pursued the bishop, a grin spread across the man's face as he moved his queen deep into enemy ranks. His opponent's king sat tucked between a pair of pawns that had once defended the monarch, yet now served as executioner's aids as the game finally ended. Braxton had won.

As the man let out a lengthy sigh, the pieces vanished from the playing field, and a small compartment opened in the center of the table to reveal a small fragment with gold and carbon etchings on its surface. Braxton picked up the piece and carefully tucked it into his coat. The man couldn't decide whether he felt defeated or victorious as the game had taken its piece out of Braxton who thought he might burst a blood vessel if the antics continued much longer. All that Braxton had to do now was figure out where his next surely infuriating test would be by talking to Heidi. After pushing in his stool to the short table, he walked up front to find Heidi, reading an encyclopedia, with her feet propped on a small stool. She looked up from the text to address the mentally-exhausted man, "If you'd like to come back tomorrow and try again, you're more than welcome."

Braxton scowled at the woman and her snide assumption, "I beat it. I've got the piece."

Heidi nearly fell off her chair as she shifted in disbelief, "You what?"

"I beat it. The game is through."

Heidi looked at Braxton with a look that bordered admiration and skepticism, "Nobody has accomplished that feat in decades if not centuries, and you mean to inform me that you are the victor of ages."

Braxton procured the fragment from his pocket and set it on the counter. Heidi rubbed her eyes and removed her round glasses to behold the phenomena that sat and stood before her. In awe, Heidi congratulated the man and opened a drawer to find a small golden key. The key went to the safe on the wall that was hidden behind a painting of a gargantuan castle that was in some far-off land. She had attempted to open the safe countless times when she had first purchased the store from its previous owner, yet she had never succeeded. A hint was scrawled across the safe that read, "An unlikely victor shall open doors for himself."

Heidi knew no unlikely Victors or victors aside from the one standing right in front of her desk. She revealed the hidden safe to the man and gave him the key to attempt to open it. As Braxton turned the key in the ancient lock, clicking noises from within the safe signified that the mystery was about to be solved. After years of waiting, Heidi anticipated the wonders or secrets that the safe might hold. However, the contents of the lockbox were underwhelming at best. All that sat in the cold steel box was a piece of parchment that had slightly begun to yellow as it had inhabited the safe for quite some time. Braxton took the piece of paper and read what was written on the handmade parchment:

Towers Rise as Rulers Fall,
He Who Clutches The Knight's Crest Shall Soon Know All,
Ascension Up Stairs Beyond The Castle Gate,
Where A Traveller Is Sure to Meet Fate

Braxton and Heidi both looked puzzled as they finished reading the foreboding poem. The castle that was likely being referenced was the one on the painting that now swung loosely. According to the embossed plaque, the castle he was looking for was Portsmouth Castle. Braxton remembered that the landmark used to be a highly decorated fortress outside of Asheville. The castle was a few miles south of the town on a hilltop that overlooked the vast sea. Nothing had been heard of the place, as the battlements had been rumored to have crumbled to dust long ago and no man dared to venture into the alleged haunted ruins of the once revered castle. Braxton had a new destination and all that was left to do was to explore the remnants of grandeur to find his next fragment. After folding the piece of paper, he placed it in his pocket and retrieved the first fragment from the counter. Heidi had returned to her encyclopedia amidst the disappointment of the wall safe. While he collected himself and his things, Heidi glanced at the man who had both made and ruined her day with his findings. After bidding the bookkeeper goodbye, Braxton and Galileo set off again down the trail towards Asheville once more. Wheels turned and snow crunched as the next chapter of Braxton's journey began to unfold before his very eyes.

Chapter Eleven

Towering Ambitions and Crumbling Realities

There was one word to describe the lengthy voyage to Asheville from Havenstein. Cold. Not the kind of cold that is welcomed after a hot summer's day or the cold that keeps one's drink refreshing. This cold made one wonder if the blood that ran through their veins would freeze over or if a new ice age was about to occur before one's shivering self. The man was bundled in everything he could manage to the point where he resembled a coat rack with his furs and fabrics layered upon his skin. No matter what he did, the cold lurked within him.

As wintry fields and bare trees passed by, Braxton pitied himself and tried to warm his hands by rubbing his gloved mitts together to little avail. Galileo seemed to be struggling in the heavy air as he intermittently gasped for some salvation in this frosty hell. After much internal griping, Asheville came into view as the sun had completely set, being replaced by a full moon that peered out from behind a set of clouds. Slender icicles hung from the storefronts, awaiting the proper city-dweller to impale. Most windows were ablaze from nearby hearths or candles that labored to keep the inhabitants of the homes and businesses warm. Braxton sought his own cozy haven in a local inn that had a fire lit in the lobby fireplace. The sleepy innkeeper paid Braxton no mind as he warmed himself next to the heavenly embers. With his fingers and toes unthawed, Braxton got himself a room and retreated to the woolen covers of an upstairs bedroom.

In the morning, Braxton awoke and headed downstairs to leave for Portsmouth Castle. Before he set out, he went across the street and had a blueberry danish and a cup of black coffee at a quaint cafe. While he was in the cafe, one of the few patrons caught his eye. A man sat in a corner with ink-blotted papers spread in front of him like a literary charcuterie board. He was presumably working on the world's next greatest masterpiece, one that would go up on every reader's shelf and collect dust with all the other prolific works of mankind. The writer didn't seem to wish to be bothered, so Braxton left the man to his own devices. With his pastry and brew in hand, he set out to the castle in the warm morning sunlight. A faint breeze blew down the street, an absolute delight compared to yesterday's arctic inferno.

The castle was only a few miles away, but Braxton didn't have the slightest clue as to what he would find at the site. There wasn't much that could surprise the man at this point after his encounters with some of the average folks that had led him onward. As the wagon drew nearer to the castle, there wasn't much to behold aside from an eroded rampart and the remains of the main structure. Cool winds whistled through the vacant corridors and studies as Braxton entered the abandoned fortress. A rusted suit of armor, once a lord or knight's prized possession, stood guard in a hallway that led to what formerly was a throne room. Tattered tapestries and broken balustrades adorned the balconies that overlooked the room. A rusted sword leaned up against the throne, robbed of its valuable gemstones, that still remained in the room. Braxton wandered through more hallways that were occupied by relics of the past and forgotten possessions until he reached an intact spiraling staircase that led upwards.

Following the instructions of the message from the bookshop, he began to climb the stairs, curious as to what "fate" awaited him at the top. When he reached the landing at the top, the man had crawled up three stories of stone-slab stairs. An intact door and a strange rug that had little knights and swords embroidered into it were all that the man found as he triumphantly groaned from the newfound ache in his joints. Braxton gently rapped on the mysterious door. From inside the chamber, the sound of someone shifting and footsteps assured Braxton that he was not alone.

Sir Edward Caldwell stood at his loom making his latest creation of carpet making. He nearly dropped his needle and thread as he was startled by a knocking at his door. The rugmaker put down his tools and tread lightly across his other fanciful carpets towards the door. Edward had never been paranoid, but he was always wary of the possibility of a phantom or ghoul serving him an unfriendly eviction notice. For safety purposes, the man drew his sword, a blunt weapon that hadn't seen a whetstone in quite some time, and opened the door.

Braxton thought that this journey had run out of tricks and awing novelties. He was wrong. The man that stood before him looked like a cross between a disheveled tailor and a confused squire with pins protruding from his pocket square and a sword in hand. The room behind the strange man was littered with a plethora of colorful fabrics and finely crafted rugs that adorned most of the floor and parts of the walls. Both of the men looked equally surprised to see each other.

Edward issued the first question between the pair, "Who are you and what in the world are you doing here? I don't suppose you've come for a decorative rug or a welcoming mat."

"Not exactly, I've come to ask you about something that I've been told you know of. Do you know anything of the *Book of Knowledge*?"

Edward had not heard that title in a while. "Well, I know of it and that a fragment of some relation was kept here long ago; however, the piece has long since wandered off to further lands. What might you want with such an item?"

"I've been searching for the book to help me find myself. If you'd like proof that I'm serious then let me show you something."

From his jacket pocket, Braxton produced the first fragment to the man who looked equal parts puzzled and amazed that such an item was before him.

Edward briefly sputtered and then responded, "It would appear as if you are sincere, but I can't offer you much more than the last place that I knew of the second fragment's keeping. To my knowledge, the piece was last given to the son of Duke Wallace, the former ruler of this castle. I believe the piece is in the possession of a man by the name of Pierce Wallace. That is, unfortunately, all I can tell you though. You've made it this far; therefore, I do believe you'll be more than capable of figuring out how to obtain the second fragment. So, unless you're interested in a rug, I've got no more business with you."

Without a farewell, Edward closed the door and went back to weaving and threading his masterful works of art. Braxton found that going down the staircase was much easier than climbing up as he descended and began walking back through the halls. A torn picture in a gilded frame leaned up against a rotted barrel caught Braxton's eye as he walked towards the front gate. The picture was faded, but the image of a man with dark hair and a plush beard could be made out despite the water damage and mold that had begun to disintegrate the paper. A scratched and chipped plaque on the bottom of the frame was inscribed with the following title: Duke Samuel Wallace, The Fair Handed.

Braxton imagined that Duke Wallace was just as charitable as his son was, but all the man had to show for his generosity was a rotting estate and an overlooked reputation. The place had once been one of the finest castles in all the land, yet now it sat in a heap of rubble that reflected no elements of its past life. It would turn out that poor misfortunes do indeed transpire for even the kindest of hearts and gentlest of hands.

These notions made Braxton wonder if Pierce would have the same story or deviate from the beaten path of his father. Only time would provide an answer to this hypothetical query that for one man was a very tangible reality. With his thoughts aside, Braxton set off once more for the extravagant paradise of Merchant's Grove to meet a local legend. The snow had begun to melt under the sun which left only icy remnants and chilled puddles for Galileo to tromp through. For lunch, Braxton had himself some hearty afternoon air and a few slices of bread that would be better described as large croutons.

As the afternoon went on, Braxton watched the sun drift through the sky until it began to set. The illuminated streets of Merchant's Grove came into view as the sun dipped below the hills. The streets were less crowded as it was the middle of the week and the temperature had dropped substantially to the point where a three-piece suit would no longer suffice as warm clothing. The street vendors had fled to the indoors as well with no tents or canopies being present on the cobblestone streets. Pierce's mansion was fittingly located in the center of town surrounded by a black wrought-iron fence. Braxton approached the front gate where a guard was sleeping on a stool with his rifle leaned against the post next to him. Since the snoring guard looked comfortable, Braxton opted not to wake him and slipped through the ajar gate. Braxton walked up the driveway where a frozen fountain was the centerpiece of the roundabout in front of the looming building. On the front doors, a pair of lion-head door knockers surveyed the happenings of the front drive. After straightening his jacket and dusting off his trousers, Braxton tapped the door with the knocker.

Chapter Twelve
The Philosophies and Fallacies of a Philanthropist

The front door opened, flooding the front stoop with warm light and the gaze of a servant. Wearing a red dress shirt and a pair of black slacks, the servant eyed the man that stood before him prior to speaking, "What business do you have here?"

"I've come to talk to Mr. Wallace about something I think will pique his interest. If you'd be so kind as to grant me council with the man, I'd greatly appreciate it."

Just as Braxton finished his statement, a melodious voice interrupted the exchange. As the servant stepped aside, Braxton came face to face with the most powerful man in Merchant's Grove, if not the greater area. Pierce Wallace stood in a well-tailored three-piece suit with an unlit cigar occupying the corner of his lip. The man radiated with the feeling of importance and lavish cologne that made one feel as if they were about to meet the most pretentious man to ever walk the earth. This hasty assumption was far from correct.

Pierce Wallace didn't carry himself as some haughty political giant or a snobby aristocrat, but rather, he seemed like a common man that merely dressed in a fine suit and a pair of fuzzy slippers. Even wealthy people apparently couldn't stand to always be troubled by the discomfort of dress shoes.

Pierce took over the questioning of Braxton, "What might you have that may interest me, my dear boy?"

Braxton responded, "I've heard that you know something of the *Book of Knowledge.*"

The cigar from Pierce's mouth nearly made its escape as Pierce's eyes went wide. Pierce seemed halfway between shock and intrigue at what the scruffy man before him had just stated. He collected himself and cleared his throat, "I may, but we should continue this conversation in a more private setting away from prying eyes and eavesdropping ears. Please come with me to my office if you would."

In silence, Braxton followed the man up a marble staircase and through a heavily decorated hall to a sizable office that overlooked the back of the estate. Pierce took his position in his red executive chair that slightly squeaked as it absorbed the man's weight. Braxton sat in one of the smaller chairs that sat opposite Pierce. The side walls of the office were lined with shelving that held an array of books and trinkets ranging from a miniature globe to a small tusk comprised of ivory. Pierce fiddled with a pen that rested on his desk as Braxton made himself comfortable. After setting down the pen, Pierce resumed their conversation, "What might you wish to know about the *Book of Knowledge* that you believe holds some unique relevance to me?"

"I'm led to believe you possess a fragment of the Knight's Crest."

"Well, you're somewhat right, my boy, but I do not have access to what you desire. The piece has been enclosed in this vase for quite some time."

Pierce produced a small vase that had white and blue flowers painted on the side from beneath his desk. "This vase is filled with gold coins with the piece laying at the bottom of it. It was given to me upon my father's demise. The vase cannot be shattered, and the coins cannot be held for they are illusions made of acid. I've tried to retrieve the piece before but if you turn the vase upside down then you will find that an endless stream of tainted gold will flow from its slender opening. There isn't much I haven't tried with my bandaged hand being the resultant of my last experiment. The only clue I was provided was the inscription on the bottom."

Pierce tilted the vase so that the message on the bottom became visible. The inscription contained three simple words, "Wealth is poison." Braxton thought back to Pierce's father who had found out this statement was absolutely truthful. Wealth has the power to erode people who seek and possess it, for jealousy corrupts the soul as much as selfishness does. Money does not solve all of one's problems because there are certain things that cannot be bought and sold.

Braxton responded to Pierce's explanation, "Would you be willing to grant me the vase, so that I may try to figure it out?"

"I will grant you this vase under one circumstance and one circumstance only: you bring me the Book of Knowledge when you find it. I have no malicious intentions toward you or anyone else, but there is something that I must know. A question I've been pondering for years, but I will not disclose it to anyone. If you trust me and accept my terms you may take the vase."

"So you wish to reap the rewards of my labors?"

"Don't look at it that way, my boy. I'm giving you something you'll need to get what you desire with only a little reimbursement for myself. A single answer is all I require. Now, do you want to come to an agreement or childishly cheat yourself out of your only opportunity?"

"I'll accept your terms, for it would appear I've got no other options. I must know one thing about you though, Mr. Wallace. How have you procured your abundance of wealth?"

"A magician does not reveal his gimmick and a gambler never shows his hand. However, that kind of question is one I'll humor for the sake of our blooming partnership. How do you believe I've amassed my fortune, some Robin Hood act where I fleece my fellow businessmen and grant the spoils to the impecunious masses or perhaps you think I was born with a silver spoon jammed between my lips?"

"Not exactly what I had in mind, but it's a sheer curiosity of mine. I don't believe many folks in this town are too tight for money, nor do I believe you conduct underhanded dealings. Your claim to fame is merely a feat that I wish to shed light on to pacify my inquisitive mind."

"Well, I'll give you a chunk of knowledge that may be able to allow you to sleep easier. I've gotten much of my fame and wealth from investments in land and coal mines. At one point in my life, I owned a quarter of the land in this town as well as almost every operational mine shaft over in Blackstone. Most people in this town will remain stagnant due to their obsessions with petty luxuries and the finer things in life. I removed myself from that group of elitists whose lives revolved around expensive booze and the most recent fashion in favor of pursuing bigger goals for myself. Complacency is a disease that has crippled our society and eroded some of the most brilliant minds known to man. We go on believing that we have it made for ourselves only to have higher successes right beneath our uppity noses."

"So, you mean to tell me that wealth is the lubricant that keeps our society running and developing, yet it is also the faulty cog that hinders its prosperity and efficiency?"

"Precisely, my boy. Those with wealth and success often don't realize there is more to garner from this worldly oyster that remains plentiful for all parties. There is little reason for most to continue to toil and labor towards another success when they can recline their plush armchairs and have another sip of dry champagne as an alternative."

"You seem to know what everyone else should be doing; however, I don't see you chasing opportunity's tail in your fuzzy slippers and silken robes. Donating money and giving theatric speeches does nothing more than provide the illusion of productivity. While your charitableness is admirable, you seem to have fallen into the very trap you have described for others. The only difference between the common businessman of this town and you is that you can identify problems. Despite this advantage, you squander it in the flashiest of fashions like the world's shiniest coin plunging down the same slimy abyss as all the other corroded and tarnished coinage."

The wealthy aristocrat shifted uncomfortably in the cushioned chair, "You may be right, my boy. If we are all inherently crippled by this trait of foul contentment then it would appear that there are no winners to behold, yet there may be some who have not lost quite as pitifully as the rest. I strive not to carve some perfect masterpiece out of this world, but I do intend to leave a small marking to show my presence once occupied some space in this eternal merry-go-round. If you are to waltz away from this conversation with anything, just know that there is always more to be had, regardless of materialistic bliss or financial freedom. I do believe there exists a place beyond the garden gate of complacency in which we may all find something that brings us true happiness."

These remarks reminded Braxton that the man before him may not be the pompous centerpiece of Merchant's Grove, but he may rather be the humbled adhesive that keeps this place from falling apart at the seams with sensibility. He could see why people could listen to this man ramble for hours. Regardless of the predispositions one may carry for Pierce, you could be assured that the man simply made sense at the end of the day. As Braxton collected his findings, Pierce opened a desk drawer and produced a small coin with his face on it and a small bit of text that had the Latin phrase "Carpe Diem" in raised lettering. Pierce passed the token across the desk and explained, "This is one of my personal trading items. It is pure gold and worth a great sum, yet I feel you will find more value in it than any swindler or salesman I've given others to. I encourage you to keep it as a symbol of my gratitude and a reminder of our arrangement. As for the remainder of the night, I've set up a room down the hall that I hope will be to your liking. I've also put your steed and wagon into my stable. Of course, if you'd rather sleep in your wagon, you are more than welcome."

Snowflakes had begun to race by the window in the office. Braxton appreciated the gesture and contemplated how bitterly cold it was outside versus how cozily warm it was in the grand mansion. "I do believe it's a bit cool outside, so I'll take you up on your kind hospitality."

"Splendid, I'll have Lucas show you to your room. He is the same gentleman who greeted you at the door. If you need anything, there is a silver bell on your nightstand that can be rung to request assistance. You can leave the vase in here or take it with you. Either way, you'll leave with it tomorrow and continue your quest."

With that, Lucas opened the office door and motioned for Braxton to come with him. The room that Braxton was shown to blew him away. Everything in the room seemed expensive from the linens to the furnishings. Even the floorboards seemed to be made of imported mahogany. As Lucas left, Braxton found a robe and other garments laid out on his bed that all fit perfectly. Braxton didn't know whether to be impressed or slightly creeped out. He set aside his worries and remembered how tired he was which oddly never crossed his mind while he sat across from Pierce. The man eventually succumbed to his drowsiness.

In the morning, the room was as it was left, aside from the smell of freshly baked rolls and the aroma of coffee hanging in the air. Braxton dressed and rang the bell for assistance. Lucas showed up in his usual attire with an apron over the top from assisting with breakfast service. The pair walked downstairs to find a grand table set with every delectable pastry, jam, and egg dish one could imagine. If heaven was earthly, Braxton was positive that this was it.

At the head of the table, Pierce sat talking to a gentleman in a pair of dress slacks and a button-up. A vacant seat beckoned Braxton to sit next to Mr. Wallace. Braxton gave in to the temptation and sat next to the wealthy man who was pouring himself a glass of apple juice as he eyeballed a plate of fruit-garnished crepes in front of him. Pierce averted his attention to Braxton as he sat down to eat. Braxton's goal for the morning was to fish out another lead from Pierce to hopefully continue his journey. Pierce started the exchange, "Good morning, my dear boy. I hope you found everything to your liking and can find something out of this vast spread to enjoy."

"Everything has been quite satisfactory, thank you. I'll get to the point of the last thing I need from you, for I believe you are much obliged to grant me this as it suits both our interests. Do you have any further leads as to where the next fragment is being kept?"

"It would appear we are both in luck then, for I do have a hunch on where the next piece is. It isn't a place that is any bit welcoming or charming. The next piece belongs to someone who hasn't gotten much liking for me or any other clean-cut politician. You'll have to coax the next piece from a prisoner. Your next destination is Holcomb Penitentiary over by Hawthorne which is overseen by Mr. Blair. I wish I possessed a more favorable lead for you, but I have faith that you can pry the piece from the rough, remorseless hands of a convict."

Braxton knew the endeavor wouldn't be as simple as playing chess and chatting up politicians, but he loathed his next scenic adventure. Rather than make his displeasure felt, he took his annoyance out on a cinnamon roll.

Chapter Thirteen
Chains of Thought and Reason

The rest of breakfast consisted of Braxton sampling everything from one end of the table to the other without much more chatter with Pierce who became distracted by other diners. Braxton finished his second plate and finished off the last of the orange juice that loitered in the bottom of his glass. After his stomach had enough, he got up from the table and thanked Pierce for his hospitality and other graces with a handshake. Braxton returned to his room to gather his things and found the blue flowery vase sitting menacingly on an empty chest at the foot of the bed.

With his few possessions in hand and in a small sack he'd found placed on the bed, Braxton departed from the estate and stole a last glance at Pierce before leaving. Pierce flashed a trademark grin and then went back to humoring whatever businessman he had ensnared in conversation. Braxton went to the stable to find his wagon and Galileo had been taken care of and were ready to depart. Lucas sat nearby on a stool twiddling his thumbs. Braxton thanked Lucas for his help to which he received a simple reply from the young man, "You're going to need all the help you can get. Take care."

Braxton wasn't unnerved by this statement, for he understood that this journey wasn't going to get any easier any time soon. In fact, the worst was probably yet to come, but Braxton was prepared to overcome whatever curveballs came his way. The wagon started off down the cobblestone street with the vase's shiny contents enticingly jingling. The fresh powder had already been removed from the streets, but every frosted window and snowy yard made Braxton feel as if he was wandering through the world's most extravagant snow globe. Hawthorne would come into view by nightfall at this rate. The temperature danced around the freezing point as the wagon rumbled through the countryside, leaving shallow tracks in the snow that had blown onto the rural trails.

The trip was quite uneventful aside from a couple of wagons passing by and a pair of cardinals sitting in a treetop. Hellfire Swamp had frozen over with the entire area being turned into the world's largest ice skating rink with large stones and trees jutting out from the frozen surface. A few children were doing figure eights and playing tag on the ice as their parents watched from the shelter of a nearby wagon. Hawthorne looked as lifeless as ever with its bleak streets that had somehow become even more deserted in the winter season. Braxton knew where Holcomb Penitentiary was because he had delivered bundles of straw there when he had worked for a farmer one summer during his youth. As Braxton moved through the streets of Hawthorne, he noticed a bulletin that was crowded with wanted posters, both old and new. Rusty nails and pins held the posters in place as a slight breeze ruffled the papers. He had a feeling that one of the stern-looking criminals would be about to have the delight of being visited by Braxton. About a mile outside of Hawthorne, Holcomb Penitentiary came into view in all its bleak glory. The structure looked like a miniature castle that looked in slightly better shape than the one Braxton had previously visited. A pair of stone-faced guards flanked the doors with rifles slung across their backs and arms folded in front of them. Both men wore matching bomber jackets that had silver badges of authority pinned to them. They both appeared unbothered by Braxton until the one to the left of the door spoke up in a gruff voice, "What business do you have here, traveler? I presume you aren't here for room and board."

The guard on the right snickered at the other's musing while Braxton responded, "I need to speak with the warden if I may. I've got business with someone who is incarcerated here."

The guard on the left volleyed back an expected response, "And why should I do this for you? What's in it for me?"

Braxton checked his pockets for anything of value and came upon the golden coin that Pierce had given him and the poker chip that still remained in the lint-ridden space. "It appears I have nothing much to offer you aside from this poker chip. It probably has some value to the gambler I got it off of."

The guard looked intrigued and inquired further, "And who might this man of mystery be?"

"I believe the man's name was Kingston Devalve."

The guard's mouth went slack as his eyes widened with intrigue, "You mean to tell me that you've got a poker chip from Kingston Devalve? He was a friend of mine from when he was locked up here back when I first manned this door. Any friend of Kingston's is a friend of mine. I wonder what ever did happen to that sly fellow. I'll show you to the warden's office."

"So it is settled." Braxton pocketed the coins back into his coat and followed the man through the iron doors that swung inward as the guard proceeded through them. As the pair walked down the hall, the guard hummed faintly to himself amidst the howling screams that came from down the hall and the sobbing of some sorry sap who apparently realized where he was for the foreseeable future. Chains rattled as prisoners peered through their cell's bars to catch a glimpse of the new face that had entered this concrete hell. The inmates wore an assortment of crooked grins, maddened eyes, and desperate hands that shook the iron bars that kept them in. After they ascended a small staircase at the end of the hall, the guard opened a door with a brass doorknob to reveal the warden's office, complete with a frowning aged man who Braxton inferred was Warden Blair. What was left of the man's hair was a frosty white, but he seemed in fantastic shape for a man of his year. The man looked up from a paper to greet the newcomer, "Who might you be, son?"

The guard exited and closed the door behind him as Braxton spoke to the warden, "I'm Braxton Sterns, sir. I'm here because I'd like to seek counsel with one of your inmates."

"You weren't sent here by Pierce Wallace, were you?"

"Actually, I was. Is there a problem?"

"Very much so, young man. Anyone who would touch Pierce Wallace with a ten-foot barge pole has no business with me. Why on earth should I grant you what you seek?"

"I'm here on my own accord, sir, but I must admit that Mr. Wallace was the person who sent me here."

"Well, which is it? Are you here for yourself or are you here to do the bidding of the lout they call Pierce Wallace?"

"I'm here for my own sake then I suppose."

"Good answer, I'd refrain from affiliating yourself with Pierce Wallace if I were you, for the man's name doesn't carry much respect outside of his little village. The man must want something of you if he helped you whatsoever. So, what agreement did you make with him?"

"I told him I'd meet with this prisoner in exchange for some information. I have no further business than that with him."

"Well, you're already on the hook, so I might as well help you unbind yourself from the anchor that Pierce is. I'm guessing you're going to want to speak with James Wallace."

Braxton had no idea of who that was or what his relation to Pierce could be, but he was positive that it was a start. A start of what he wasn't sure about. The warden got up from his desk and took Braxton back downstairs. They walked for a bit, passing through halls of rowdy prisoners and outstretched arms. A silence fell upon Braxton and the warden as they passed through a door into a separate block with mostly empty cells. The warden stopped in front of a cell that was decorated with hand-made pottery and other luxuries that had no business being in a penitentiary. A man sat on a cot with his head in his hands. Unlike the other inmates, the man was dressed in fine garments and looked of sound mind. An eyepatch covered the prisoner's left eye. The warden punctured the silence as he unlocked the rusty cell door, "James, you have a visitor."

The warden locked Braxton and James into the cell together and exited the cell block without another word. James looked up to address his unlikely visitor, "Who are you?"

"I'm Braxton. I've been sent to ask you about something. What do you know of the *Book of Knowledge?*"

"I know that the text has brought suffering to many, including myself. Who sent you to do this?"

"Pierce sent me here."

"My brother cannot leave me be, even when he has everything he wants. The items you see in my cell, with the exception of my pottery, are attempts at him trying to drive me mad by giving me a morsel of my old life. If you were sent by my brother, then I'm assuming you want the piece of the Knight's Crest that is in my possession. I'd happily bestow such a burden upon anyone, but I shall relinquish it under a couple of circumstances. The first would be that you are not to give my brother the book even for a split second when you find it. Secondly, I want you to burn the book after you've gotten what you need from it, so this grand scheme can finally end. Any objections?"

76

"I must ask you one more question about something that your brother gave me. He gave me a vase that he claims holds the second piece of the crest, is that so?"

"Absolutely not, I designed the vase that you hold now with the assistance of a mage who has long since turned to dust. There is nothing in the vase aside from a distraction and suffering for curious hands. My brother probably still has the piece hidden in the locked drawer that is in his desk. He most likely intends to deceive you into retrieving all the other pieces only to stab you in the back when it suits him. Now, do you accept my terms?"

"One more thing, if you would. Don't you wish to escape this lavish prison and go live in the outside world?"

"I have no desire to leave this place, for I have seen the horrors and uncertainties of the world. I've watched good men die and corrupt scoundrels amass fortunes that are unimaginable. My eyes have beheld all they wish to see, for I cannot look into the eyes of a starving pauper while I know my brother and his colleagues feast away at their plentiful table. I can't be a part of a world where gnashing teeth and vengeful fists have overtaken the virtues of kindness and empathy. This state of solitude has allowed me to be content in a time where it seems that even the richest of aristocrats cannot seem to afford the simplistic commodity of contentment. Till my end, I will remain here. Now, if you haven't got any more philosophical quandaries up your sleeve, do we have a deal?"

"We do. I'll ensure that the book never is stained by your brother's pampered fingers, and that the book is soundly destroyed after I find what I need from it."

"Well, now that you've asked me an onslaught of questions, I feel I've got one for you. Why do you want the Book of Knowledge?"

"I feel that you've helped me find my true reason for seeking out this talisman, for even though I can see my surroundings, I've been a blind man. I've wandered aimlessly for so long that I hoped this journey would give me more purpose in life, even if my purpose is to find this book and destroy it and then wither away in my own state of isolation."

"A noble cause you are. The piece that I have for you is in that small pot in the corner. The next person you'll have to seek out will be an old friend of mine over in Westfield. He's a retired sea captain by the name of Bernard Winthrop who spends most of his time people and boat watching from his little bungalow's porch. He's the next step towards getting the next piece."

Braxton walked over to the dusty corner and picked up a vase that was decorated with stripes and chevrons. He tipped the pot and out fell a piece that looked much like the one he had acquired in Heidi's bookstore. The edge of the piece was smooth with the inner edge having indents and intricacies like a gilded puzzle piece. When Braxton turned around, Warden Blair had unlocked the cell door and was waiting for Braxton to emerge. As Braxton and the warden walked down the hall, James bade the traveler farewell with a simple line, "Till next time, my friend."

Chapter Fourteen
A Seafarer's Serenity

After leaving the Holcomb Penitentiary, Braxton recollected himself and took inventory of his wagon. Braxton had enough food to last him for another stint as well as enough fresh water stored to keep him hydrated for quite some time. As Braxton looked over the assortment of odd items he'd acquired on this journey, he couldn't help but reminisce on the faces he had met and the places he'd been. He wasn't quite sure if he was fond of these people and their quirks or simply intrigued by their atypical personalities. The poker chip which he acquired from Kingston in Havenstein was the piece that started his bizarre collection of wonders and knick-knacks. Asmodeus's ominous masterpiece still sat in the wagon, wedged between the side of the wagon and a small crate. Just looking at the foreboding image sent a shiver down Braxton's spine. His next adventure brought him to the doorstep of Merlin, a man who could be politely referred to as eccentric. He'd received nothing but a bit of advice and a lead from the man, not counting the image of Merlin in his undergarments that would forever be ingrained into Braxton's mind. After his traumatic visit with Merlin, Braxton had traveled through the mountains to seek out the Keeper, who he now knew as Horace Walker. Horace had sent him to his niece Heidi, but Braxton had strayed from the path and went to save Kingston and Sean from the cleaver-wielding maniac by the name of Foster. After a brief house call in Foster's Grove that resulted in Foster and Kingston's cowardly demise, Braxton and Sean returned to Havenstein and parted ways.

Braxton's attention was stolen away from his reflections by the cawing of a raven in the lofty branches of a tree which made Braxton's heart leap. After that brief heart attack, he returned to his recollection of memories from the last few weeks. The journey trudged on as Braxton ventured to Heidi's bookstore to acquire the first piece of the Knight's Crest which was guarded by a kingdom of chess pieces. After defeating the game, he traveled to meet a rugmaker who had set up shop in an abandoned castle. Edward Caldwell had been the person to send Braxton into his current predicament, the family feud of the Wallaces. Pierce Wallace was the next piece in this vast and perplexing jigsaw puzzle with his neatly combed hair and an award-winning smile. Pierce had given him the flowery vase, which was apparently just decorative and deadly, as well as the coin that currently dwelled in his coat pocket. The information from Pierce led him to the place he currently tarried, Holcomb Penitentiary. Braxton had met James Wallace, Pierce's brother, who made a pact with him to destroy the book and to slight his brother and his malevolent intentions. At the end of all this madness, Braxton had two of the five pieces he needed and was on his way to find out about a third. The finish line of this endeavor was not anywhere near, but it was there and that was all that mattered to Braxton. Time is only as valuable as the actions that consume it.

Braxton continued to take inventory before heading off toward the small fishing town of Westfield. He found a few oddities that he wasn't aware were with him from a crate of miscellaneous books to a deck of tarot cards that preached wayward omens from their illustrated fronts. As entertaining as rummaging through his wagon was, Braxton knew he had better be on his way to Westfield if he wanted to arrive by tomorrow morning. The path to Westfield would weave through the rolling hills that covered the expanse between Hellfire Swamp and King's Crossing. King's Crossing was less of a town than just a few cottages and shops situated around a well-traveled section of road. The road from King's Crossing to Westfield was impeded only by the Node river which pierced through the flat stretch of land. Braxton took his caravan through Hawthorne once more and proceeded towards the East. The hills were mostly covered in pastures and meadows that wooly sheep occupied. At this time of year, the creatures looked like plump summer clouds that had sprouted legs and began to graze and wander the countryside. Galileo seemed to envy the lush, warm coats of the herds of sheep.

The trail had become a bit muddier as the snow began to slightly melt which didn't improve the ease or pleasure of traveling as the undercarriage of the wagon and Galileo's legs had become caked with dirt. Braxton couldn't complain too much as the winter season had driven all the pesky insects from the atmosphere, ensuring that Braxton wouldn't have to deal with any air raids from blood-thirsty mosquitos. The air was cool but not unbearable, permitting travel to be conducted in a semi-comfortable manner. King's Crossing came into view as the sky began to darken slightly. The main structures of the small town consisted of a sweets shoppe, an inn, and a blacksmith shop that were huddled together on a corner of the crossroads. The lights in the candy store were illuminated as a man in a white apron labored away to make the colorful candies and rich chocolates that were sure to bring a smile to local children's faces. This carnival of lights was an illusion to distract customers from the atrocious amount of money they were about to spend there. Rabid children and annoyed parents didn't care for the pricing as both parties were willing to shell out the funds to acquire a moment of bliss brought to them by their local sugary swindler.

Braxton watched as the man behind the counter stretched and pulled a golden paste until it seemed to extend the whole length of the counter. Hungry and dazed from his travels, Braxton's last wit of intuition told him to continue on towards the inn to feast upon whatever morsels were left in his wagon. The plentiful feast of that night consisted of a pear and a few pieces of dried venison jerky that had been packed away in a side compartment of the wagon. After tethering Galileo behind the inn, Braxton went inside and got himself a room. The rest of the night was a blur as Braxton passed out after a groggy series of vivid thoughts plagued his mind for a short while. These wild and short-lived thoughts were unmemorable nothings by the next morning.

After a good night's rest, Braxton awoke to the reverberating clanging of metal next door and the chipper chirping of birds from the rooftop. Braxton got dressed and headed out into the morning light. Eager to arrive at his next fateful encounter, Braxton got the wagon set and headed out of town. The small village of Westfield was only a couple of miles away. Once one travels into the Northwestern region of the Great Expanse, the hills become dotted with nothing more than small flocks of sheep and gypsy camps occasionally interrupted by a small settlement such as Westfield. These settlements were occupied mostly by shepherds and fishermen who had found peace in the green pastures or on the sandy shores. Some folks didn't need to overcomplicate their lives.

A small gathering of bungalows came into view as Braxton passed over the crest of a hill that now revealed the alcove that was hidden between two cliffs. Braxton scanned the front porches of these residences until he came upon a weathered man sitting in a rocking chair, smoking a cherrywood pipe. The man's house was painted a vibrant orange that mixed nicely with the yellows, blues, and greens of his neighbor's homes. Braxton parked his wagon under the branches of a bare oak tree and walked towards the porch-dwelling sailor.

Bernard Winthrop was a man of simplicity in his seaside fortress of tranquility, also referred to as a waterfront bungalow. After retiring from sailing a decade ago, he had elected to enjoy his retirement by basking in the morning sunrises and savoring every draw from his pipe. He sought no grandeur or wonder aside from what lingering before his front stoop. On this peculiar day, wonder presented itself in the form of a young man with an exorbitant amount of questions.

Braxton approached the ex-sailor's porch and greeted the man, "Good morning, sir. You wouldn't happen to be Captain Winthrop, would you?"

"Perhaps I am. Who might you be?"

"I'm Braxton Sterns. I've come to ask you about something that I've been told you're knowledgeable of."

"You must be Pat's boy then. Your father and I go way back. I'll tell you what I can, but how about we do it over a nice cup of coffee."

"Sure. I suppose I could go for a cup if you're offering."

"Then it's settled, coffee first. Questions second."

The old man stood from his chair with a brief wince and proceeded through the front door. Braxton followed the sailor into his brightly colored home for a cup of coffee and answers pertaining to the everlasting endeavor Braxton was burdened with.

Chapter Fifteen
The Brewing of Coffee and Storms

As the smell of dark roast coffee filled the air, Braxton and Captain Winthrop's conversation also began to occupy the salty sea air that lingered in the quaint bungalow. The pair of well-traveled men sat at a small table with their cups filled with caffeinated nectar as they began to talk about Captain Winthrop and Braxton's father's glory days sailing on a ship called the *Downeaster Alexa* across perilous seas and through pirate-infested isles. These tales of yore amused Braxton, for his father had apparently left out this chapter of his life when telling stories to Braxton. Prior to finding his passion in clockmaking, Braxton's father had worked every job under the sun from glassblowing to ironwork, so the fact that he was once a sailor came as little surprise to Braxton. After a series of probable tall tales and fables from his days at sea, Captain Winthrop addressed the elephant in the room, for Braxton had certainly not traveled this far to simply listen to an old geezer ramble about his prime. "Assuming I have what you need, what information can I offer you?"

"I've been told you know something of the Knights of Dark and the *Book of Knowledge?*"

"Ah, yes. I know much of the Knights of Dark, for once upon a time I was a member of that group of secretive night owls. I hope you haven't gotten yourself tied up with the Wallaces yet, or you might have a better fate jumping head-first from one of the nearby cliffs onto the jagged rocks that line the shore. Those brothers have more blood on their hands than a congregation of butchers. I've not dabbled in matters relating to the *Book of Knowledge* in quite some time. What might you wish to know about such matters?"

After taking a brief sip from his mug, Braxton gave an explanation, "Well, I'm led to believe that you know the location of a fragment of the Knight's Crest."

83

Captain Winthrop let out a brief sigh, "It would appear that you're already too invested to back out now. I presume you've already made introductions with the Wallaces and another old friend of mine, Horace Walker. I pity you, for not even the largest wave I've beheld could wash out all the corruption and delusion that you've been engulfed in. The best advice that I can give you at this point is trust no one because even the purest of souls have something they'd like to pry out of the *Book of Knowledge*. Seeing as you've come this far, you must have something about you that wills others to aid and trust you. Turning you away would do you no favors, so I suppose my decision has been made for me. I encountered the crest fragment on an isle that lays a few miles off the shore from this alcove. I speak of the Isle of the Iron Bell, inhabited by a cult of fishermen who refer to themselves as the Harbingers that have isolated themselves from the rest of the world. When I last visited the isle, I discovered that the leader of these so-called Harbingers had the piece hung around his neck by a piece of twine. These strange islanders are welcoming to newcomers, but they are quite pious and skittish when it comes to outside influences."

"So, the only way to reach this island would be to sail there?"

"Yes, that would be the only way. I'd be willing to take you, but I would like something in return. This isle is not only home to a bunch of deranged doomsday conspiracists, but it also is the only place where my favorite coffee bean is native to. Gilded Mocha Beans have only been known to grow on that small island, therefore, I'd like you to return with a bag of coffee beans as well as this sacred fragment of the Knight's Crest."

Braxton was slightly baffled that he wasn't being roped into another backhanded deal where he would need to destroy a magical talisman or put it in the hands of the greatest conman to ever plague Merchant's Grove. "That's a deal I'll make. When should we depart?"

"Once I finish my coffee, we may. My sailboat is down by the water at the end of my dock. You may want to dress warmly for this ride, for it will be no sunshine-filled expedition."

Braxton finished the remnants of his coffee and walked outside to the wagon. Braxton found a jacket that was lined with fur and had a rough leather exterior that made him look like an eskimo. After putting on his boating attire and feeding Galileo one of the last apples from the wagon, Braxton wandered down towards the dock that protruded out into the icy shoreline. A paper-thin layer of ice covered the shallow shore, serving as an opaque barrier between the fish who dwelled in the water and the eagles who sat perched on a root that hung from a cliffside. The eagles seemed quite glum and defeated that nature had closed their seafood buffet, but they observed Braxton with great intrigue.

Braxton turned back towards the bungalow to see Captain Winthrop making his way down the rocky shore toward the dock. The man walked with a severe limp that was moderately aided by his cane. This was the man that Braxton was about to trust with his life at sea. Braxton came to terms with the fact that this very well could end poorly, and he hoped that the reaper had his scythe freshly sharpened if things turned sour.

The old man finally made his way to the dock and began fiddling with ropes and cables until the boat was tethered by a singular line. As the ship bobbed in its idle wake, the pair boarded the ship. Captain Winthrop adjusted the sails and undid the last rope, assuring Braxton that it was indeed too late to reconsider. The ice cracked and popped under the bow of the small vessel as it lurched toward the open waters. Without much delay, the eagles swooped down to take their pick of the fish that had lost their icy protection. Braxton couldn't help but feel a little guilt as he watched the astounded fish wriggle in the beaks of the majestic fowl. Perhaps the consequences of Braxton's actions were not solely imposed upon him.

After leaving the shelter of the cliffs, Braxton began to shiver as the winds began to chill him to the bone, regardless of his fur-lined coat. As the shore disappeared and water stretched to the horizons, thunder rumbled in the distance.

Chapter Sixteen

For Whom The Iron Bell Tolls

The still waters eventually became more lively as the sky darkened with storm clouds that hovered above. Amongst the rambunctious waves, the sailboat was tossed about like an ingredient in the world's largest salad. Captain Winthrop seemed energized by the storm, for he seemed to chuckle faintly as he navigated the restless waters. Braxton tried to follow Captain Winthrop's brief instructions and loosening some ropes while tightening others, unaided by the water that was persistent on soaking everything in the vessel. While Braxton struggled, Captain Winthrop continued to maintain his composure, despite the fact his drenched beard was starting to develop icicles. As lightning continued to strike and thunder continued to roll, the ship kept its course until all that was left of the storm was light freezing rain and a few waves that disturbed the glossy surface of the sea. Through the distant fog, Braxton could make out a small island that was presumably their destination, based on the fact there were no other land masses within a square mile of them. A monastery stood stoically at the highest point of the isle with Braxton being able to distinguish a few smaller structures surrounding the grand centerpiece.

Braxton still wondered what he was in for, so he pried for more information from the seasoned sailor who currently looked fresh from the arctic circle with his icy beard and frosted eyebrows. "So, who is the leader of these devout loons, captain?"

"He goes by the name of Brother McGuffin, but I don't know much of what he looks like, for everyone dresses the same in this civilization. You'll be looking for a man in a brown cloak that is bald is about all I can tell you which narrows down the choices from a hundred to about eighty."

"Well, I'll take all the help I can get, I suppose. Anything else you can tell me about him or these nutcases that may come in handy?"

"Not really. It looks like they've redecorated a bit since the last time I visited though."

Braxton turned to see that the village was not as peaceful as he had once perceived as a few of the thatched roofs were blackened and smoldering from being lit ablaze. A few barricades made of carts, boxes, and sandbags could be made out on the edges of the grouping of homes. Something was not right.

Captain Winthrop eased the boat towards the shore until it glided on a bit of pale sand and halted. He proceeded to drop the anchor onto the sandy beach to ensure the waves would not repossess his watercraft. The pair forfeited their soaked jackets for warm coats that were produced from a sealed compartment in the boat that had apparently been unfazed by the frenzy of water that had bombarded the deck. After loading their pockets with snacks and a bit of gold, the pair made their way toward the carnage. They made their way up a slender dirt trail until they came to a barricade that was manned by a pair of malnourished men who looked like a hearty gust of wind would blow them out to sea. Each man wore a brown cloak with a white stripe down the center of their hood. The one on the left hefted a large spiked club that looked like it might do some damage to a vulnerable cerebral cortex while the other reached for a flintlock pistol that was holstered at his belt. The man who spoke didn't exactly have the voice of an angel by any means, "You there! What business do you have here?"

Captain Winthrop spoke up for the pair, "We're here to seek out the leader of the Harbingers, Brother McGuffin. We intend to do no harm."

The gruff man with the club stared coldly at the pair for a second before barking out, "Reya!"

A woman stepped through a gap in the barricade, wearing a similar robe to the guards, except her stripe was golden. She looked like a precious flower among the chaos and smoke that had blanketed this place. Her voice flowed like silk from a spinning wheel as she addressed the strange newcomers, "What might you require from Brother McGuffin at this dire time, gentlemen?"

Captain Winthrop continued to speak for the pair as Braxton tried not to stare at Reya or lock eyes with the stocky guard who still remained at his post. "We've come looking for something that the honorable man knows the whereabouts of. If you could grant us counsel with him, we'd be greatly in your debt."

"I'm afraid I couldn't grant you this privilege as the rebels have taken him hostage as some ploy to try to overturn the power dynamic of the island. He's most likely being kept at the monastery that they've claimed from our grasp."

"If we help you guys retrieve Brother McGuffin, would you allow us to have a private word with him?"

"Certainly, I'd be more than happy to grant you that if you can aid our cause. We were intending to make a push towards the monastery this evening under the cloak of night to hopefully surprise these radical rebels."

Braxton hadn't the faintest idea of what time it was, but he assumed it was getting late in the afternoon as the men had been at sea for quite the spell and the sun was beginning to dip below the water. Braxton finally spoke up before Captain Winthrop could continue, "We'd be more than obliged to assist you however we may."

"Splendid, you're more than welcome to join us for dinner, but I should warn you. We don't have much selection."

Braxton and Captain Winthrop followed her to a fire that had a few crates, boxes, and stumps scattered around it to form some sort of makeshift gathering place. Looking around the fire, the sights were grim to say the least. A man who was missing an arm sat on a stump eating from a dented can that was wedged between his knees, wielding a tarnished silver spoon in his remaining hand. Another man wore a robe that was coated in blood which unnerved Braxton and made him a tad bit queasy. The person who sat to the right of the amputee was reading from a small book through the one lens that remained in his glasses. An assortment of arms was scattered about, ranging from a hunting rifle to a set of daggers that were stained with dried blood. The embers of the fire seemed to be the only lively attendee of this depressing pow-wow with its dancing flames and encompassing warmth. As the sun sank below the horizon, Braxton and Captain Winthrop feasted on their own can of beans and oranges that had certainly seen better days.

As the sky began to darken, Reya began to explain the infiltration plan to Braxton and Captain Winthrop. There would be a firefight that would be used as a distraction outside of the front entrance of the monastery. While the distraction played out, Braxton, Captain Winthrop, and Gunther would flank a small side entrance to the building. Braxton learned that Gunther was the friendly club-wielding person he had met at the gate who was now assigned to ensuring that the newcomers didn't get any grand ideas while carrying out the plan. Braxton was to be armed with an old long rifle and a dagger while Captain Winthrop had apparently supplied his own blunderbuss that had been kept on the inside of his coat. Gunther would be armed with his beloved mauling club and a hunting rifle of his own. The crackle of the fire gave Braxton the feeling that, much like the sparks that leaped from the blaze, he too, had no idea where he was about to end up.

As everyone gathered their arms and supplies, Braxton and Captain Winthrop sat alone at the fading campfire with their guns loaded and pockets filled with pouches of gunpowder and bullets. Reya eventually summoned everyone to the barricade that sat only a few hundred yards from the front steps of the monastery. She seemed to have a way of leading that left nobody with any second guesses and with a boldness that invigorated those around her. Before leading her troops into battle, she dispatched the infiltration party to take the trail through the seaside underbrush to get to the side entrance. Gunther, Braxton, and Captain Winthrop crept in silence through the underbrush until they came to a parting of two scraggly trees that revealed the side door. As they all hunch over to get a glimpse of the guard who manned the door, all hell broke loose on the other side of the monastery as gunshots and cries could be heard over the crashing of waves on the shore. The young guard at the door had become distracted by the disruption and paid the prying eyes of his true assailants no mind. This particular guard was armed with a rifle and a sword that hung from his belt. As the guard peered around a pillar of the monastery to catch a glimpse of the conflict at the front steps, Gunther made his move. Braxton jumped as the sound of a rifle discharging sounded over his shoulder. After his ears stopped ringing, Braxton looked to see that the curious guard was now slumped on the ground next to the pillar, blood oozing from his lip and the new wound in his chest. The trio exited the bushes and cautiously approached the door. No one else seemed to be near as everyone's attention seemed to be fixed on the main assault at the front of the structure. Gunther led the men through the door into a hall that led only to a bare storage room and a flight of stairs that spiraled upward.

The three infiltrators gingerly proceeded up the stairs until they reached a balcony that overlooked the central area of the monastery. An ornate golden dial made up the central area of the main floor with foreign runes carved into its surface. A black obelisk dominated the center of the dial with its dual peaks reaching for the starry sky above that peeked through the opening in the domed ceiling. Braxton's attention was immediately drawn to a group of people who surrounded a man who was tied to a chair at one edge of the dial. A tall, stocky man in a plain brown robe, devoid of any stripes, faced the bound man who sat in the chair. The sound of the man who Braxton guessed was the leader of the rebellion chimed through the vast chamber.

"...You believe this petty war your misguided supporters are waging is going to get us anywhere? These people are only playing themselves as they proceed through this gauntlet of defiance and rejection of what will bring about a better tomorrow. Your days of misleading these helpless lambs into your snare of greed end today. I'll grant you one last chance to renounce your faith of lies and deceit and come clean to these people you've hurt. What will it be, become a martyr of your misdeeds or become cleansed of your trespasses against the people of this island?"

Gunther aimed his gun at the rebellion's leader and awaited the perfect instant to pull the trigger when the man stood still. Brother McGuffin issued his response from his bondage, "You already know my answer. You'll gain nothing from killing me aside from the pleasure of knowing you've silenced one more voice that knows of your delusion. Even if I confessed, I'd be torn to shreds by the masses for what I've done."

The leader addressed his prisoner once more, "So, is that a yes or a no, Brother McGuffin?"

The drained eyes of Brother McGuffin glared up at the face of his captor as he delivered his final response, "I'll perish as a man of good faith. May god help..."

Brother McGuffin's response was abruptly cut short as a bullet pierced his chest. However, the shot had come from above. Gunther had shot him.

Every head in the room turned to look for the culprit until everyone looked at the same man. The leader of the rebellion looked to be in shock as he called out to the man on the balcony, "Who has purged this holy site of the wretched soul of Brother McGuffin?"

Gunther addressed the rebels from the gallery, "I did. This charade had to come to an end, and that man was merely prolonging his own selfish plot. I've had suspicions of the man for quite some time and it appears the misdeeds have finally caught up to the manipulator."

The leader of the rebels looked like he'd been vindicated as someone else had discovered what he had already known: Brother McGuffin wasn't quite the upstanding man he'd been made out to be. As Brother McGuffin gasped for his last breath, the iron bell that hung in the tower of the monastery rang out over the distant sounds of war.

The leader of the rebellion was the first to infringe upon the silence that had fallen upon the monastery, "We must stop this senseless violence immediately. There need not be another drop of blood spilled over this cowardly conman."

Braxton, Gunther, and Captain Winthrop all proceeded down the stairs to the main floor and now stood at eye level with people who were their enemies a matter of minutes ago. However, they were all part of the same cause now as they had found the wolf amongst the sheep. The men ran outside to cease the fighting, but Braxton lagged behind, for he remembered why he was there. Brother McGuffin's face was pale and he was still bound to the chair with a series of ropes. A thin strand of rope ran around the man's limp neck that had allowed his head to tip forward. Braxton was no coroner, but he believed that Brother McGuffin wouldn't be causing any more conflicts anytime soon. As he untied the necklace and pulled it from the man's neck, a medallion surfaced from the man's tattered robe. The shiny gold and glossy black etchings assured Braxton that he was one somber step closer to his fate.

Chapter Seventeen
Another Brick in the Wall

The aftermath of the battle was far from what anyone could deem glamorous or mildly discomforting. In the glade that stretched before the monastery, bloodied bodies leaned against makeshift barricades as the smell of gunpowder lingered over the hallowed ground. All the surviving members of both sides now stood in the middle of the field, surely debating their own futures. Braxton found Captain Winthrop who was standing next to the leader of the rebellion.

Kellen Gastieu felt as if he'd made a round trip to hell and back, without accommodations, in the last couple of months. He'd established himself as the leader of a rebellion that had intended to quickly oust the corrupt leader of the Harbingers. This intention was far from what reality had in store. Brother McGuffin had been selling out every item of value from the island to a man by the name of Pierce Wallace. Kellen had served as the financial advisor to Brother McGuffin for years when he stumbled upon something he most likely wasn't intended to catch wind of. Numbers came up short and certain exports just overtly went missing which didn't bode well for the former leader of the Harbingers. A monumental problem now stared Kellen in his green eyes: how does one put a civilization back together? Something told him that it would take more than all the king's men to put this humpty dumpty of a society back together again. This undertaking would not be completed without time, for these people needed to repair more than just shattered windows and singed thatched roofs. Bonds would need to be amended between people who had fired upon their former friends and stared into the maddened pupils of their families over the last few months. As it would turn out, war was hell.

The pair of outsiders left the group to their own devices and headed back for the mainland. Braxton was caught up by Captain Winthrop on the boat ride home on what had occurred briefly after a ceasefire was called for by both sides. Kellen Gastieu had been voted the new leader of the Harbingers almost unanimously shortly after the fighting stopped. Some people who were backing Brother McGuffin still had mixed feelings about the outcome of the dispute, but they seemed to be making quick strides towards acceptance. Captain Winthrop didn't get his coffee, for he didn't anticipate it was appropriate to request a sack of coffee beans from the war-torn islanders. He'd have to make do with the grounds he could get from the general store. The whole journey wasn't a loss, however. Aside from the ending of a civil war, Braxton had gotten the third fragment of the Knight's Crest.

The notion that his three fragments were surrounded by gimmicks, conflict, and deceit made Braxton wonder what other wonders he was in for to acquire the last two pieces. He'd have to pay Pierce one more visit, but he hadn't the slightest clue as to where the other piece could be. As he looked out over the calm waters of the sea, it felt as if the whole world was taking a moment to assess what it had just beheld on the Isle of the Iron Bell. After taking in this serene instance, his mind began to race: *Maybe he was simply just another speck amongst the rest of the world. Or possibly just a mere piece in a grand jigsaw puzzle containing millions of other nondescript pieces? Or was he just another hopeless fly trapped in an intricately woven web, composed of chicanery and empty promises by Pierce Wallace?* These questions made Braxton unsure of whether his sanity was fleeting or if he was just beginning to come to his senses of his situation.

To distract his mind from this cosmic quandary, Braxton tried to coax information about the next piece from the weathered, cracked lips of Captain Winthrop. "So Captain, do you know anything of any of the other fragments or their bearers?"

As he worked on adjusting the sail, Captain Winthrop responded to Braxton's seemingly spontaneous question, "I know not much more than I've told you, my dear boy. The best advice I can give to you would be to seek out your father, for I believe he knows more than he's ever let anyone privy of. That man knows secrets that nobody else could even fathom."

Braxton couldn't believe the fact that his dad, of all people, was somehow entangled in this mess because Braxton believed his father to be a simple clockmaker without much intrigue. Then again, most tend to forget that there was a time before them in which their parents actually did more than just sit around and read the paper and oversee the doings of their children. There was never an inclination within Braxton to question his father about his past, for he believed that all his father had to offer were tired stories of his glory days and tall tales of his youth.

Braxton's train of thought became derailed when he realized that the sailboat was now docked at the small pier just behind Captain Winthrop's bungalow. As Captain Winthrop tethered the boat to the rickety dock, Braxton stepped off the watercraft. The sky had already begun to darken as the pair of weary sailors returned to the seaside residence's porch. A silver crescent moon peered down from behind a pair of gray clouds. Stars began to poke holes of light through the bleak veil of night as Captain Winthrop and Braxton gazed up to the heavens from their rocking chairs. A raven stirred on a nearby gnarled tree branch. Braxton fought to remain awake while Captain Winthrop somehow seemed more lucid than ever after his bout at sea. The crisp evening air assisted Braxton in propping his eyelids open while Captain Winthrop took puffs from his pipe. Braxton soon felt ready to proceed onward toward Longwood, so he bid the Captain goodbye and promised to visit again some other time as he continued off down the trail into the night.

Chapter Eighteen
Wagon Wheels and Lucrative Deals

T he wagon rambled on for quite some time until Braxton could see King's Crossing in the distance. Braxton almost dozed off to sleep with the reins in his hands until a wheel encountered a cavernous pothole that triggered a raucous sound from below the wagon. As he stopped the wagon, Braxton imagined that one of the wheels was just in need of a bit of grease or a pesky nail or bolt had popped out of place. He was far from correct.

When he went to investigate the damage, Braxton could see that the back wheel had fully been snapped at the wooden spokes from the impact. Wood splinters protruded from the spot where the bottom spokes had once been. With this news, Braxton found himself stranded a few miles from the nearest town in the middle of winter. Due to his lack of better alternatives, Braxton set up camp for the night with what few supplies he had left. He managed a lamentable fire and blocked the open ends of the covered wagon with plaid sheets. His campsite would've been laughable to most, yet it was ample enough to keep the man alive. Galileo had been tethered to a nearby tree and given the biggest blanket that Braxton had. At least the horse was content in its multi-colored quilt.

For dinner, Braxton dipped into his pitiful stock of canned goods from which he ate a tin of pears and a can of beans that had been unsuccessfully heated over the fire. Despite his lukewarm beans and vehicular misfortune, Braxton was happy with what little he had out here in the middle of nowhere. After the grueling day he'd had, Braxton found no difficulty in allowing his eyelids to clasp shut.

Braxton awoke to find that the sun had emerged from its cloak of clouds, allowing for warm sunshine to flow over the frozen Earth which had already begun to thaw. These rays of heavenly grace allowed the traveler some element of comfort. As he began to pack away the blankets and quilts, he heard the sound of another wagon approaching over the hills. The wagon that approached looked oddly familiar to Braxton, who was not quite fully awake yet.

The driver of the wagon clinched a briar pipe between his lips and one of his hands that clutched the reins was wrapped in gauze. Braxton couldn't tell whether the universe was playing some kind of cruel joke on him or if he had simply managed to break down at a scenic vantage point of the valley below. Whatever it was, Braxton now came face to face once again with the colorful artist that had taken up temporary residence outside of Longwood. Asmodeus had stumbled back into Braxton's path.

The wagon parked next to Braxton and the painter hopped down from his driver seat with a friendly smile on his face. "Morning stranger, looks like you've got yourself quite the predicament."

"Indeed, I do. You wouldn't happen to moonlight as a wheelwright would you? Or might you know someone who can lend a hand?"

"I'm not handy myself unless you're looking for a painting of a wheel. Wits aside, I do know a man who may be able to help you. He's a woodworker from King's Crossing who might be able to fix your small issue there. The man is an old friend of mine, a matter of fact, he makes all my easels. I'm sure he can craft something for you on short notice."

"Well, I may be able to slowly rumble into King's Crossing on the three wheels I've got left. I hope you're not in much of a hurry to get anywhere."

"Not really. I was on my way to Westfield to see if I could draw some inspiration from the magnificent cliffs that guard the shoreline. The cliffs shall still be there tomorrow, I hope, so I've got no confliction with lending a hand. We can depart now if you're ready."

"Sure, just let me get my things packed away and we'll give it a run."

Braxton packed away the last of his campsite and hitched Galileo back to the crippled wagon. As it started to sluggishly move, Braxton's optimism began to sink like an anchor with every pop and crack that he heard from below. The wagon teetered and groaned as it proceeded down the rough path toward King's Crossing. Asmodeus's wagon chugged along behind Braxton as the town began to come into view. Fortunately, Asmodeus's friend lived on the close side of town, for Braxton feared the wagon would be a pile of scrap lumber if it had to endure much further. The homestead was a modest dwelling with a small home that was dwarfed by the red barn that stood in the backyard. As Braxton pulled his wagon, creaking and grinding included, into the barn, a short and gruff man emerged from the backdoor of the home.

Oliver Wainwright was not expecting a visitor on his day off. He'd been sitting in his kitchen having a glimpse at the local paper as he heard a cacophony of what could be gently described as a proverbial train wreck. He sat down his mug of orange juice and went out to see what the cat had dragged into his barn. The cat in question was a man who stood at six foot with a slender build that had what once might've been considered prim attire but was now marred by dirt, dust, and lord knows what else. His wagon looked as disastrous as Oliver had assumed.

The smell of sawdust and musty hay hung in the barn as Braxton was approached by the squat man. Asmodeus had parked his wagon next to the barn and joined Braxton inside. From what Braxton could see, the barn was stocked with every sawblade one could need as metallic blades hung from hooks on the wall like an armory for a small militia of lumberjacks. What looked to be the start of a small skiff hung from a pulley system that was suspended above the main floor. The scents and saws reminded Braxton of his childhood when he would accompany his father to a lumberyard, that was now long gone, over by Longwood to pick up materials for his latest ornate timepiece. Much as the lumberyard itself, these days were long ago and long gone.

Braxton's reminiscing was interrupted by the greeting of the woodworker, "Good morning, gentlemen. What can I do ya for?"

Asmodeus looked to Braxton who issued a response, "The spokes on one of my wheels seem to be broken, and I'm in need of a quick fix. My friend here says that you'd be able to help me out."

Oliver looked to Asmodeus, "Ah, well I appreciate the referral, my friend. I wouldn't hold your breath on a finder's fee though."

Oliver bent down next to the wagon to inspect the damages to find that wheel was as good as toothpicks. What once were spokes were fractured ends with only two of them remaining intact. It was a miracle that this heap of cloth and wood had made it here from any distance.

After his evaluation of the marvel, Oliver informed Braxton that he would need an entirely new wheel, for the one he currently possessed was kindling at best. Braxton reached into his pocket to produce the funds for the new wheel, but all his hand could grasp was some lint and a small pebble that had somehow made its way into his trousers. Braxton's luck had run out.

Oliver raised an eyebrow, "Out of change, are we? I don't suppose you've got something you can put up for collateral considering you're in a rush."

Braxton rummaged through his pockets until he came upon an unlikely savior. Ebner's silver pocket watch. The watch was sterling silver and had to be worth a fine penny, but Braxton was reluctant to hand over such a keepsake as temporary payment. Ebner would've thought of Braxton as foolhardy if he didn't make what seemed to be an obvious deal. If Braxton played his cards right, he'd be able to reclaim the watch once he paid his dues to the woodworker later. Braxton produced the watch from his pocket and presented it to Oliver. Oliver's eyes went wide as he addressed the timekeeping masterpiece before him, "Now that's something. I'll happily take that as collateral if you're willing, for this beauty must be worth quite a bit. I almost hope you default on my payment and that I can keep it for myself. I'll give you until the fourth day of December to bring me five grams of gold. Do we have a deal?"

This offer gave Braxton a little over a week to scrounge the funds together to pay the man. A grin spread across Oliver's face as he reached his hand out to shake Braxton's. After a brief moment of thought, Braxton shook the man's hand and said, "We have a deal."

"Well, this won't take me more than an hour to complete, so if you'd like to hang about my workshop here you are more than welcome, or if you'd rather wander off then that's fine with me."

Asmodeus took this opportunity to depart, considering that his presence was no longer necessary. He gave Braxton and Oliver a brief farewell, "Well, I'll see you around Braxton. And as for you Oliver, I'll be back to pick up my new easel in a few days. Take care, you two."

As Asmodeus sauntered back to his wagon, Braxton made conversation with Oliver while he began to assemble a new wheel using a set of vices and his meticulous hands. A pair of unpainted marionettes hung limply above a workbench, preparing for their grand performance someday. Intricate wood carvings filled a couple of shelves while a large carving of a knight stood stoically on patrol. The wall above the workbench was plastered with everything from small handsaws to a two-man crosscut saw that spanned the length of the bench.

Braxton and Oliver's conversation began to slip away from small talk and become one of actual substance when Braxton asked Oliver about a curiosity concerning the relationship between Asmodeus and him. Oliver hesitated to answer, but then he gave Braxton the real answer. "I've known that man for years, but our friendship is sheerly dependent upon him being a frequent customer of mine. It's all business and nothing more. He puts money in my pocket, and I repay him with easels and customer service that some may mistake for friendship."

"Interesting, I suppose that is merely the art of business. However, I can't say that Asmodeus sees things like this."

"Don't get me wrong, Asmodeus is alright with me, but at the end of the day, I've gotta make a living."

The silence that followed this exchange could've been cut by one of the saws on the wall, for Braxton couldn't help but question who his true allies were. It was difficult to discern between lip service and comradery, but Braxton seemed to have a way of bridging the gap and leaving an actual impression on people. After the morning grew old, Oliver got the attention of Braxton to inform him that the wheel was repaired and he was set to proceed on his journey. Braxton left with a brand new wheel and his mind stewing over the things he had seen and the people he had met.

Chapter Nineteen
Time in a Bottle

Braxton's journey continued homeward to Longwood on his new wheel and Galileo's hooves. After this whole quest was said and done, Braxton decided that he'd allow the industrious steed to roam free in the apple orchard to reward him with a plethora of Honeycrisps and Macintoshes. This trip seemed to have aged the pair of beaten adventurers a collective decade in the last couple of weeks. Nonetheless, the wheels continued to turn and Galileo continued to trot.

Hellfire Swamp still remained preserved in ice as the caravan passed by the lackluster waypoint once more. No children lingered on the ice, but a few signs of the visitors remained. Abstract shapes had been scratched into the icy surface of the swamp by a pair of razor-sharp skates. A wicker picnic basket had been abandoned in a nearby snowbank while a crude snowman stood forlorn, awaiting the return of its companions. This somber scene seemed to be frozen in time aside from Braxton's intrusion.

Drummond Manor sat in its usual place with decorations being put into place for the approaching holiday season of yule. Braxton observed as he watched Theo clumsily hold a ladder as Lac stood atop it, attempting to hang holly from a balcony. This circus act seemed to be semi-successful as strands of the festive shrub had already been hung on a few other railings and windowsills. Garrison North seemed to be also taking in the spectacle as he stood guard in front of the main entrance that had been decorated with a pair of evergreen wreaths. Braxton imagined that Lord Cardoff Drummond sat inside by the fire, wrapped in lavish blankets and sipping rich hot chocolate.

Meanwhile, Braxton was out and about traveling the wintry world and enduring hurdle after hurdle. Comfort was a luxury that Braxton couldn't afford at the moment, for he possessed nothing of value to put up for collateral a second time. When he reached Longwood,

Braxton began to fumble through his mind for a way to subtly ask his father about the next fragment of the Knight's Crest. As it would seem, it was hard to make such a monumental subject into simple small talk.

His parents had retreated inside for the winter with the wispy strands of smoke slithering out of the chimney being the only sign of life within the residence. Children romped through the snowy streets in wool mittens and heavy boots, toting arm-fulls of snow to strengthen their forts and fashioning a stockpile of snowballs to unleash upon their neighbors. These shenanigans would certainly result in parental intervention when someone inevitably would take a projectile to the face or lob a chunk of ice at another youth. For now, laughter and playful shouts filled the streets.

Braxton parked his wagon before his parents' home and got down from the driver's seat that had not gotten much more comfortable since the first day of travel. He knocked on the door and waited on one of his parents to answer. Dressed in a white blouse and a pair of blue jeans, his mother opened the door and was greatly surprised and slightly skeptical to see her son back at their doorstep after such a brief hiatus. "Well! What a pleasant surprise! What brings you back so soon, dear?"

"I've got some things I've gotta ask dad about. Is he home?"

"Of course he is. He's taken up residence in his recliner in the living room that he so fondly adores. Do come in." As the pair walked down the hall to the living room, Braxton's mom fussed over his attire and offered him some leftover coffee from that morning.

Braxton stepped into the living room to see his father reading the paper and smoking his pipe, because what else do retired men have to do? His father sat up in his chair. A fire dwelled under the mantle that had been adorned with three stockings and a strand of garland. Patrick sat down the paper to address his son who undoubtedly was here for something since he had visited more than once in the past three months. Braxton sparked the conversation, "I ran into an alleged old friend of yours over by Westfield the other day. A man named Bernard who claims you two have quite a bit of history together."

"Ah, yes. I haven't heard that name or seen that face in quite some time. How does he fare these days?"

"He seemed quite well, but you never told me that you were a sailor at one point."

"I suppose I didn't, for tales of raiding ships and hoisting sails never did seem like much of a good bedtime story. For what it's worth, I did sail for a good while with Bernard back in my twenties and thirties when I possessed a bit more energy and desire to travel the globe. I traveled to many lands and met many people. I perpetrated my fair share of good deeds and misdeeds, but it was simply a means to make a living. Your mother convinced me to settle down when I was thirty-three and that was the end of my sailing days. How did you run into that ancient seadog?"

"Well, it's a long story, but you may know something about what I've been up to. Bernard said you know something of the Knights of Dark and the *Book of Knowledge*."

"I don't know why you've stuck your nose into this matter, but I do know of these subjects of which you speak."

"I'm assuming you know what these are then." Braxton produced the three pieces of the Knight's Crest from his coat and set them on the coffee table. His father looked upon him with a look between amazement and horror.

Patrick's eyes widened as he took in what sat before him. "I have not the slightest clue how you've managed to get these items. This should be an impossibility, yet here we sit. I suppose you're here to unearth the location of one of the other pieces, but I should inform you that someone else is out to find it as well. Pierce Wallace was here earlier this week and tried to smooth talk and incentivize me into telling him of the location of the unknown piece that you both seek. I suggest you leave the pieces you already have with me until the time comes to use them or else I speculate that Pierce will have some underhanded way of taking them from you that you may not like."

"I suppose you're correct, but how am I supposed to know that you're not about to sell the pieces to him regardless?"

"Braxton, that crook has taken more from me in my life than I care to admit. I don't plan to take a small payout from that sleaze to cut my losses after all these years. I'd like nothing more than to behold his fall from arrogant grace."

"What kind of history do you have with Pierce?"

Patrick let out a sigh and told a story he'd never told anyone before that hadn't lived it with him. "In my youth, I worked in many different odds-and-ends jobs until I began working on ships. I met Bernard when we were both working in a shipyard prior to our endeavor as sailors. The two of us ended up working as hired hands on a ship by the name of the *Golden Asp* that was captained by the man in question. Pierce was nothing more than another urchin clinging to the deck of a ship that had been financed by his father when I met him. After a few years of rolling barrels and toting crates, Bernard and I had amassed enough funds between us to make a proposal to Pierce. We offered to go into business with the young aristocrat and split the profits and expenses between the three of us. Pierce accepted this deal, but he had other ideas in mind of how he was going to maximize his profits and cut his losses. The folly he'd committed was what created the everlasting rift between us that still lingers and stings like the remnants of salt that still festers in an infected wound. With no concept of long-term consequences, Pierce decided that it would be best to begin smuggling illegal goods to add a bit of side profit for himself to partake in. However, when you begin taking jewels and art pieces from royals, you are destined to be caught. Pierce read the writing on the wall and decided to sell us out to the foreign royals he'd been stealing from, so those wronged nobles promptly boarded our ship and captured Bernard and me. Within the week after our capture, some anonymous "Robin Hood" paid off the family and allowed us to walk with no physical wounds to show, but we both had a new chip on our shoulder. I suppose the moral of this story is don't waste your time with the wrong crowd."

This story of years gone by made Braxton ponder just how Braxton was using his own. He wished he could bottle his precious time and stow it away in his cellar. When he went to uncork it, would it flow out rapidly like bubbly champagne or seep out flatly like syrupy molasses? He would never know, for time couldn't be contained or stopped by anything, much less a wooden stopper. Braxton could hold onto his time spent, however. He'd have enough stories and memories to fill every glass bottle on the face of the earth. Braxton set down his racing thoughts for a moment and continued his conversation with his father, "It would seem that not too many folks have had a positive experience doing business with Pierce Wallace. I'll leave these three fragments here with you while I seek out the fourth one, but that begs my next question of you, dad. Where is the next fragment?"

Braxton's father took another puff from his beloved pipe and answered, "It's been many years since I last laid eyes on the fragment and the man that guards it. The man who possesses it has been written off for many years by most of the world aside from the distant few who know of his whereabouts. He's a man by the name of Cliff Straus who lives in an old estate over by Ramstead. From my knowledge, he lives in what used to be a lavish estate that has now been overgrown by greenery and ivy. He still remains there from what I know, but I don't know if he's alive yet. Nobody has stepped foot on the estate for quite some time after Cliff sealed the gates shut almost ten years ago. The man must be in his late seventies now. Oh, how the time flies." Patrick looked almost wistful but continued nonetheless, "If you continue down the main road of Ramstead you are sure to find the estate in its natural state of disarray."

"Well, I'll let you know how he's faring if I find him. I evidently missed out on quite a few stories when I was younger. I know I probably don't say this enough, but thank you, dad."

Braxton didn't know if he was expecting his father to shed a tear or get emotional, but his father remained in his state of mild intrigue even though Braxton was positive he had struck a chord with his old man. There was still business to be attended to and roads to be traveled, so Braxton made sure his father put the three pieces of the Knight's Crest into a secure safe that had been stationed under his father's desk since Braxton was a little boy who would play with the dial. Braxton headed back out into the cold streets, despite his mother's insistence that he eat something before he left. Galileo stood right where Braxton had left him.

Braxton figured that he ought to stop back at his cottage to restock his supplies and get some clean clothing. He couldn't believe he had been on the road for weeks. He was tired, but he wasn't finished. With his path set in front of him, Braxton set off for a place he hadn't been in quite some time, home.

Chapter Twenty
A Crown of Thorns

Pierce Wallace sat at his desk, sipping from his favorite coffee mug. He had a meeting with all of the most powerful people in the Great Expanse in a matter of minutes, and he knew what fate lurked on the horizon for him. His debt was about to come due, and he was penniless. Perhaps they'd pity the man and grant him a bit of amnesty, or at least enough time to get his hands on the *Book of Knowledge*. This was less of a friendly luncheon between chummy businessmen and more of a feast of cannibals who were seated opposite of each other, evaluating their next victim. Lucas appeared in the doorway, and Pierce couldn't conclude whether he was being led to a new opportunity or to his execution. The pair walked down the red velvety carpets that seemed a lot more foreboding than comforting now.

The Great Hall of Merchant's Grove was a warzone coated in formality and dainty hors d'oeuvres. Banners that bore the crest of the Great Expanse had been draped over every railing and balcony. Servants bustled about carrying bottles, cutlery, and new dishes to the table. At the head of the table, King Dadelus had humbly helped himself to Pierce's usual chair. Pierce was granted a seat between two people who he knew by name and nothing more. The Baron of Asheville, Callum Reaves, sat to his left while the archaic Lord of Longwood, Nigel Brahms, sat to his right. Across from Pierce, a man who was attending his first meeting as a member of the nobility seemed sheepish and more interested in the plate of food before him than the wealthy aristocrats that surrounded him. Pierce had never been formally introduced to the young chap, but he'd heard it was Jameson Drummond's boy, Cardoff, who was now sitting in his father's seat at the table after his recent passing.

Altogether, sixteen members of the nobility sat at the table with only one empty chair that had been vacant for some time. Nobody had heard from the Straus Manor in years, but many had just assumed that the whole family's lineage was wiped out after the mysterious disappearance of Clyde and Loretta Straus. There was rumored to be one member of the family left, but they'd not bothered to return any letters or summons that had been sent to the manor.

Disregarding missing attendees, business carried on as usual with most keeping their conversations to a murmur, discussing debts, loans, and favors. The magnificent spread before them was heaped with sliders, cheeses, salads, and a large roasted boar that was the headliner of the grand table. Pierce had lost much of his appetite, so he ate a small roll with some raspberry jam to chase his coffee. Some may say it's unjust and undignified to try a man for wrongdoing in his own home, but that's precisely what followed.

King Dadelus brought the table together to begin the proceedings that everyone had awaited, aside from a free meal. The stout king had a gravelly voice that filled the impressive chamber, "Good afternoon, ladies and gentlemen! We've got much to attend to, so I suppose we should get down to the matters that we've gathered to discuss. The first order of business is to address our new member who has graciously opted to join us. Lord Cardoff Drummond, the heir to Lord Jameson Drummond's fortune, welcome to the Council of the Great Expanse!"

Applause from servants and a few noblemen made it seem like they were all seated in a circus tent, watching Cardoff perform stunts and tricks like some trained seal, rather than inducting a new member into the grim undertaking of the nobility. The king continued on after this brief interruption.

"Secondly, many of us at this table seem to have a score to settle with one particular gentleman among us. The admirable Duke, Pierce Wallace, has amassed quite a debt, and it appears that he has failed to pay his dues. I will allow the charitable fellow to plead his case before I take suggestions on the repercussions of these grievances. Mr. Wallace, the floor is yours."

Pierce stood and looked at the many sets of cruel eyes now affixed on him. King Dadelus looked like he was about to take in a spectacular rendition of a play rather than the testimony of the damned. When the room fell dead silent, Pierce began his ruse of an explanation. "Thank you, Honorable King Dadelus. To begin, I'd like to thank you all for your patience and generosity in my time of need. As much as it pains me to confess, I find myself in a position that requires a sliver of extra time to amend. If I'm granted one more week to fill the demands set before me by my lenders then I will have all accounts paid in full by the conclusion of this period of time. However, in the case that I fail to heed my promises, I open myself to any consequence that may come for me. If there are any other concerns, please feel free to display them now."

A murmur came over the room as many deliberated whether or not to trust the word of the charming philanthropist. King Dadelus called the table back together for proposals or approval for Pierce's offer. The first person to request to speak was the Baron of Westfield, to whom Pierce owed a small sum of gold. King Dadelus granted the baron his request. "I feel that we can give the man another week, for none of us benefit from watching the man hang. A dead man is not capable of paying back anything. I move to approve the proposal put forth by Mr. Wallace."

King Dadelus shook his head in approval because it was evident to most that they could not beat their dues out of Pierce. A verbal vote started at the far end of the table opposite Pierce. The results of the survey were split down the middle. The Baron of Asheville, the Lord of Longwood, the Baron of Westfield, King Dadelus, the Duchess of King's Crossing, and the Baron and Baroness of Havenstein all voted to allow Pierce more time to pay his debts. The dissenters, including the deplorable Lord of Ramstead, numbered an equal amount, seven. It was a tie. Impossible.

Someone had abstained from voting and would now serve as the tiebreaker.

King Dadelus scoured the table for the unheard voice and settled his gaze upon Lord Cardoff of Hawthorne. "You've yet to voice your opinion, young man. What say you on the matter of Pierce Wallace?"

Cardoff looked up to address Dadelus. Cardoff spoke in a mellow tone that combined scholarly undertones with smooth delivery, "If you ask me to decide this man's fate before me based on the little I know, I'd say to let him walk free, for I haven't the slightest negative disposition towards him. Let's just hope that he keeps it that way."

King Dadelus looked fascinated at Cardoff's poise and tact. The boy's father would never be able to carry himself like that, for he always seemed brash and stubborn in his old age. The baffled king composed himself and clarified the new leash that had been fastened around Pierce's neck, "It appears we've reached a verdict to allow Pierce to make amends in the next week before any consequences will befall him. I do believe that is all we have to formally discuss today; therefore, let there be merriment and fine food."

As Dadelus began to mutilate a roasted chicken leg, Pierce shifted his focus to Cardoff Drummond. This young man was quite different in an intriguing yet concerning way for anyone attempting to conduct profitable business around him. At least the youthful lord had pardoned Pierce so that the debtor may be weighted down once more by his crown of thorns. Pierce was determined to turn the tables around on his seemingly grim fate. The *Book of Knowledge* would be his by any means necessary.

For the time being, Pierce chose to take this time to mingle with the nobles around him that had just saved his neck. He'd remember those who had helped him and those who'd opposed him if he lived to see another day after this week. The first people he sparked a conversation with were the Baron and Baroness of Havenstein who seemed quite chipper. The baron conversed mainly with Pierce while his wife juggled three different conversations which constantly made her head and eyes dart back and forth across the table like a goldfish that requires several different distractions to entertain its wavering attention span. There wasn't much substance to the conversation with the pair, but it reassured Pierce that he had someone on his side. The rest of the banquet was a blur as Pierce helped himself to a few cocktails and more senseless exchanges of words. Liquor flowed and so did the conversation, but none of it mattered. Everyone was here to make money and further their own agendas to add to their hoards of gold and pride. Dignity was a secondary thought when there was money to be made and smiles to be flashed.

Pierce used the festivities and chatter to distance his mind from his dire situation, for no sane man likes to fantasize and fuss over their possible last week of life. He'd already drawn up his strategic game plan to give him the best odds of obtaining the *Book of Knowledge*, and all there was left to do was execute the clever plan. Despite his limited amount of time, Pierce used the rest of the day to butter up his peers and collect himself. As his distinguished guests made way for their homes, Pierce was left alone with his thoughts and a glass of cognac. The servants toiled about clearing the table and cleaning up the bottle of white wine that the Duchess of King's Crossing had kindly dropped on the polished tile floor. Some people had indulged a bit too much for their own good.

At the end of the day, Pierce requested that no one bother him in his study. Pierce unlocked the drawer that contained one of his prized possessions, a piece of the Knight's Crest. As he moved his hands over the glossy surface of the piece, Pierce couldn't help but feel sorry for himself. His house of cards was falling and all he had left was one sorry piece of a puzzle and regret. Pierce wasn't an optimist by any means, but he had no choice but to hope for the best. His options were finite as was his time to scrounge up the funds to pay his foolish debts. Perhaps the consequence would not be fatal to Pierce; however, he knew there was nothing more that some of the nobility would like but to see him strung up or whimpering under the blade of a guillotine. Pierce decided to sleep on his complex and poorly orchestrated reality.

When he awoke the next morning, Pierce remained unbothered. He was brought a platter of items for breakfast that would've made his day brighter if it was not one of his potential last. After stomaching a couple of pieces of toast and a slice of orange, Pierce gathered himself and prepared to set out to find a man who would be instrumental in Pierce's plot. Once he had adorned his travel cloak and a few meager supplies, he mounted his black stallion and rode off into the morning sun.

Chapter Twenty-One
A Return to Roots

After staying the night in Longwood, Braxton began his journey home under the warm visage of the morning sun. The snow had melted off without leaving a trace of its icy claws in sight. As Braxton ventured his way home, he had a worrisome concern as to whether he had locked his front door before his departure. If he hadn't, his home was a playground for pillagers and squatters alike. Fears of overturned furniture and broken windows plagued the man's mind as he passed over the rolling hills. His humble cottage, seemingly unscathed, came into view as he passed over the last stretch of road. Braxton put Galileo back into his homey stable and proceeded inside. A ransacked home would've been an improvement upon what he actually found.

When Braxton proceeded up the stairs to his study, he was greeted by the warm smile of an unwelcome visitor who was seated in the chair next to his cluttered desk. Braxton addressed this intruder, "I don't remember hiring a housekeeper while I was away. What business do you have with me, Pierce?"

"You really shouldn't leave your house unlocked while you're out and about. You may let thieves or some worthless vagrant in, my boy. I'm here because you have a few precious things I want."

"All I have for you is a goodbye and a request to postpone any further visits to my residence indefinitely. You can also have your decorative vase back. What else could you possibly want with me?"

"I want you to hand over the three pieces of the Knight's Crest that you possess to me. I'd also like the location of the final piece. That is all."

"Well, what could you possibly offer me that I'd want? Despite your fine attire, you're a beggar in my house without any ground to stand on."

"I have nothing of monetary value to offer, but I do have something much better. If you grant me my request, I'll save you from the inevitable destruction that the *Book of Knowledge* will bring as well as I'll end the deceitful ruse my brother is trying to pull over on you."

"So, you mean to offer me a pair of blatant lies for my possessions? I believe you've forgotten how to do business."

"I speak of no untruths, for I received word yesterday of my brother's departure from Holcomb Penitentiary. Warden Blair has paid for this foolish blunder with his life, and I'd hate to see another life squandered due to my brother's misdeeds. It would be a pity to see you fall at his hand. All I request is that you allow me to save you."

"I trust no man. We are all subject to our weaknesses and our moments of desperation. I suppose it's not a lack of trust as much as it is an understanding of the human condition. Anyways, I will politely decline this outlandish proposition of yours."

Pierce's pleasant demeanor shifted as a frown crept across his face, "I sincerely hope that you will reconsider, for the time for sensible negotiations is coming to a close. We will both rue the outcomes of this exchange."

"I'm sure we will. I'm merely deciding between lesser and greater evils at this point, for I do comprehend the parameters in which I must operate to evade the worst. You will hopefully someday find yourself in a position where this clambering pursuit for greatness will be in vain. As you sit upon your throne of ruin, may your conscience fill with guilt, for you know not what you do nor what your selfishness does. May these thoughts find you elsewhere and not in my home. Anything else you'd care to discuss?"

"I believe that is all, for I am not here for a philosophy lesson or small talk. May fate not tarnish your righteous self. Good day, Braxton."

As Pierce left the cottage, the air seemed to thin, and Braxton was left alone with his thoughts on his own throne. The wooden desk chair was a modest throne at best. Braxton noticed something peculiar that brought a slight smile to his face, a singular owl feather that rested on his journal. He'd forgotten about the small creature who had presumably fled the cottage by now to roost in a new set of rafters. At least someone had hopefully found peace in this stony-hearted land.

Braxton's scotch glass sat on the table with an amber ring in the bottom where the last drops of the liquor had settled. His desk was still as cluttered as ever with pens, inkwells, papers, and other trinkets that reminded Braxton his workspace wasn't as put together as he was. His solitude almost felt underwhelming, but it was serene and calm. Relaxing at home wasn't supposed to be exhilarating or stressful. After all his adventuring and excitement in the past weeks, sitting at home seemed to be boring and dull, but it was exactly what his mind and body needed. We shouldn't criticize or scorn ourselves for indulging in moments of laze or idleness, for we all need to put our feet up and just enjoy nothing from time to time.

Braxton took in everything and nothing simultaneously as he sat and read from an old book that had made its way onto his desk. The book was an encyclopedia of fowl that had knowledge of every winged creature ever beheld by human eyes. Despite the thousands of other birds in the work, Braxton paused at the page that depicted barn owls. A picture of a white-feathered bird, identical to the one that once peered over Braxton's shoulder, was on the opposing page to a description of every aspect of the cordial owl. Perhaps this image was based on the same owl that Braxton had seen, and the bird was more well-traveled than Braxton had given it credit for. Birds and books aside, Braxton felt like he had begun a return to his normal life of tranquility and ease. He was aware that this feeling wouldn't last, for he had yet to fulfill his mission and there were still scores left to settle. Braxton closed the hefty book and set it back down in its place on the desk.

The afternoon had come as the morning departed for another day. Braxton planned to leave for Ramstead late in the afternoon to hopefully stay the night at the inn before investigating the situation at Straus Manor. There was much to do and much to be had, but Braxton was content sitting where he was, staring out the window at the bleak sky.

Time didn't halt for Braxton, so he figured that he ought to restock the wagon and get ready to begin again. As he rummaged through his cellar, Braxton thought about Pierce's warning. The question that truly left Braxton baffled was the debate between who was being truthful and who was not being sincere. James had never given Braxton much reason to distrust him, and for all Braxton knew James still sat in Holcomb Penitentiary in his lavish cell. Pierce, on

112

the other hand, had deceived Braxton before as well as he'd not garnered an ounce of trust from Braxton. There was only one way to find out the answers to these questions and all would be revealed in due time. After he loaded one final box onto the wagon, Braxton set off to the stable to retrieve Galileo. Once the horse was hitched and Braxton had changed into a fresh set of clothes, the caravan took off once more for Ramstead. What lay ahead was something that was both unfathomably horrific and surreally awing.

Chapter Twenty-Two
Horror Beyond Humanity

T he forest had not changed at all with its pines still deeply rooted in the soil and a distant woodpecker tirelessly working on his latest masterpiece. The trail had become hardened under the icy scrutiny of the winter sky that remained clouded yet refused to disperse any precipitation. Braxton wasn't complaining, for he'd had his fill of snow for the year and longed for the dog days of summer. Braxton would rather be wiping the sweat from his brow on a warm beach somewhere than trying not to turn purple from frostbite. The familiar inn of Ramstead stood like a stoic pillar amongst the squat cabins and cottages that surrounded it. Braxton figured that he ought to ask the innkeeper if he'd heard anything of the happenings at the nearby Straus Manor.

The gruff innkeeper sat in his usual post behind the oaken desk that overlooked the small lobby. Braxton greeted the man, "Good afternoon, sir. How are you this fine day?"

Shifting in his small chair, the innkeeper looked up from his papers and answered the inquirer, "Fine, fine. Weren't you just in here a week or so ago, young man?"

"I was, and for some peculiar reason, I find myself back in your neck of the woods. I've got a question for you if you don't mind me asking. What do you know of Straus Manor?"

"Well, that's a loaded question you've got there, son. I know much and nothing of Straus Manor that broods to the south of here. I used to cut firewood for the Straus's before their manor became shut up and abandoned. After Loretta and Clyde passed three years ago, I haven't heard anything from their boy, Cliff, in years. He was always a quieter type, though, so I suppose he wouldn't have much to say regardless. What could you possibly want from that dilapidated estate?"

"Nothing truly, just curiosity getting the best of my muddled mind. I appreciate your insight, and I'll be sure to stop in again for a stay maybe, if I find myself back here again."

Braxton left the inn with a new destination and a new acquaintance to meet. The wagon rumbled down the gravel path out of town towards Straus Manor. As the caravan went around a bend in the trail, the behemoth of masonry came into view. The place had stone walls that shielded the first floor of the residence from view, but the two stories that towered above were in full view. Ivy coated much of the barrier wall and stretched up the house's walls toward the shingled roof that looked like a carpenter's nightmare. Broken windows and a loosely-hanging gutter gave Braxton the impression that Cliff wasn't exactly into home maintenance. Braxton parked his wagon before the wooden gate that stood eerily ajar. A broken lock sat mangled on the ground next to the gate it had once secured.

Braxton cautiously walked through the gate and up towards the house that sat lifeless. As he approached the front door, a raven caw sent a jolt of fear through the man who was already unsettled and unnerved from his warm greeting to the overgrown jungle that had once been an impressive mansion. The front door was locked. Braxton decided to knock politely on the door. No answer came from within the residence.

Due to the lack of hospitality, Braxton surveyed the outside of the house for another point of entry. Oddly enough, a couple of crates were stacked before a shattered window that had been covered with a cloth for safe passage. Something was definitely amiss.

Once he hoisted himself through the window frame, Braxton was greeted by what once would've been a quaint dining area. The table was still set with champagne flutes and plates that were now adorning a layer of dust. One diner had apparently forgotten to clear their plate, for a rotten cut of meat sat next to a spoiled pile of greens that polluted the air with a putrid stench. The rancid smell was only pierced by the cold breeze that intruded through the broken window pane.

Braxton wandered down the hall from the forgotten dinner party and stumbled upon what had once been a grand study that had its walls lined with shelves and still retained the scent of old books. Stacks of books, papers, and boxes crowded the edges of the room. A large rug dominated the center of the floor in this vast room. A strange set of stains stood out on the grey rug. Braxton examined the room and found another peculiar detail. A set of shelves that hid some sort of secret doorway had been left ajar. The mysterious doorway seemed to descend down below the manor. Braxton opted to save this dark passageway for last.

After he reached the top of a spiral staircase, Braxton took in another oddity that both intrigued and daunted the seasoned traveler. A candle sat lit on a table that had become a makeshift desk for some scholarly squatter. Braxton's ear perked up as the scratching of a pen on paper could be heard. Upon further investigation, Braxton found a pair of open exterior doors and discovered a bearded man sitting on a small balcony that overlooked a hidden courtyard that was the centerpiece of the estate. The man on the balcony ceased his writing and turned to face the intruder who had infringed upon his rightfully stolen property.

Albus Weatherly had stumbled upon Straus Manor last week and began his next literary work based upon the abnormal happenings of this strange estate. Albus believed that he was divinely fated to write from a young age and had been trying to get his first masterpiece completed since. He'd written everything from poetry to memoirs of his youth, none of which had ever developed much past a few scribbles on a page. This was different though, for as he sat observing the monstrosity of Straus Manor, he knew this was going to be what he needed. Albus had explored much of the manor to get to the bottom of what had really happened to this once-revered estate. He'd found more than he'd bargained for in his snooping, but he wrote down all the horrific scenes and realities he'd observed for the sake of his work. He'd been observing the human-like monstrosity that was barbarically feasting on some sort of carcass in the courtyard when he came face to face with the first person he'd seen in quite some time. It was also a familiar face.

Braxton's attention quickly shifted away from the man on the balcony and was consumed by the beastly creature that was hunched over in the courtyard. Dark purple ulcers dotted the exposed skin of what appeared to be some sort of mutated and disfigured human. Whatever the beast was, it was still wearing the shredded remains of what had once been an olive-green suit and still had a few tufts of dark hair jutting from its head. The anomaly looked to be eating from the remains of some kind of large bird. The strange being seemed oblivious to the pair of observers that were frozen in shock and awe at what they were beholding. Albus put a finger to his lips and ushered the visitor back inside and drew the door to the balcony shut. Braxton snapped out his disbelief and interrogated the old man, "What on Earth is that and who are you?"

"You look familiar, young man. Regardless, I'm Albus. That creature is what remains of the last heir to the Straus fortune. He was once referred to by the name of Cliff Straus."

"Weren't you that writer that was in that hole-in-the-wall cafe in Asheville? And why are you here?"

"I was. To answer your second question, I found this place last week and have been writing about the oddities of this god-forsaken place. What business do you have here, for you look neither like a ghost nor a scruffy vagrant?"

Braxton paused as he eyed the man before him. After a quickly resolved mental debate, Braxton gave the man a condition of secrecy to fulfill, "Well, if I tell you the reason I'm here then you wouldn't be able to repeat it."

"I don't think I could divulge your secrets to anyone if I wanted, for not too many people want to listen to what an old kook like me has to say."

"I suppose that's fair. I'm here to look for a piece of what is referred to as the Knight's Crest."

Albus's face turned from a look of seriousness to one of intrigue as Braxton had uncovered a forgotten instance from Albus's childhood, "Ah, so you're in the hunt for the *Book of Knowledge*. My father once told me about that talisman, but I merely assumed it was some absurd fairy tale. He claimed that he'd been one of the people who created it and stowed it away. I never imagined that it was real nor that I would ever encounter another soul who knew of such things."

"So, your father must've been a Knight of Dark. To my knowledge, the *Book of Knowledge* is quite real and so are the dangers it poses. Would you be willing to assist me in finding the fragment I'm looking for?"

"I can do better than that. I have a hunch that I know where it is, but you're not going to like where. The item you seek is in the beast's lair in an upstairs bedroom on the other side of the manor. It's in a lockbox that's key is around the belt of the monstrosity. I haven't the slightest clue as to how you'd like to go about retrieving the key without sending the beast into a violent frenzy."

Braxton pondered his circumstance. He was trapped between a ruthless beast and a hard place. "I may need to think on that, but in the meantime, how did Cliff end up as this horrid creature?"

"It's quite the long story that's truly tragic, but I'll give you the short version. When Cliff lost his parents three years ago, something inside of him broke and sent him into a downward spiral of desperation and sorrow. The loss of his parents made him lock eyes with death and realize his own mortality. To spite fate and death, Cliff set out to create a serum that would grant him immortality and save him from his humanity. Cliff eventually concocted something that had never been witnessed by human eyes, the Everlasting Serum. All that Cliff knew was that the seemingly brilliant innovation would spare him from his eventual demise, but he failed to recognize the long-term consequences. The serum began to mutate Cliff's body into the mass of purple sores and grayish skin we see now. Cliff had found his deliverance from death, but he was now forced to be burdened with something that most would condemn as worse than death, eternal suffering and anguish. Addicted to the purple elixir, Cliff continued to ingest the brew due to his body's dependence on the liquid to stay functioning. There isn't a drop of blood coursing through that man's veins currently, just a lot of purple goo and regret. Now, Cliff is seldom present in that warped humanoid figure that walks these halls. Tis quite the pitiful existence for a man so well-respected and liked as Cliff. The best way to get the key you seek would be to put Cliff out of his misery. We merely have to figure out how to kill something that even death itself cannot purge from this earth. I believe the best course of action would be to see if Cliff left any antidotes or counteractive measures in his notes kept in the laboratory beneath the manor. I'd be willing to accompany you down there if you'd like."

"It would appear that is the most sensible way to go about this. I'll allow you to lead the way."

The pair descended down into the study and then down the dark staircase that led into the laboratory. Devices, syringes, and beakers littered workbenches and shelves. Some smashed glassware lay unrepairable on the floor that had specks of the purple serum spattered across it. Albus and Braxton rummaged through boxes and crates with no immediate findings. After a few minutes of digging, both of the men stopped their search and averted their eyes toward the stairwell. A set of footsteps was coming down the staircase.

Chapter Twenty-Three
Ascending to New Depths

T he monstrosity that had once resembled Cliff Straus did not look much more amiable from up close. It walked with a cane that's shaft was comprised of two snakes that formed a double helix. The silver head of the cane looked sharp and looked to be polished with what Braxton assumed was the dried blood of his latest meals. Braxton had hidden himself behind a bookshelf that had been slightly pushed away from the wall while Albus looked to have hidden himself behind a clumsy stack of boxes. There was a slit through the wood in the bookshelf that allowed Braxton to observe the doings of Cliff Straus in his underground laboratory. From his hidden viewing spot, Braxton watched as the beast hobbled over to a table that had a small syringe full of purple serum in it. Cliff let out a distorted growl through his warped mouth as he jammed the needle of the syringe into his left arm.

After smashing the empty syringe on the ground, the monstrosity's attention was beckoned by a noise that had sounded from across the underground chamber. A book had fallen off the stack of boxes that Albus was hidden behind. The creature glared in the direction of the writer. It dismissed the distraction as it staggered its way back upstairs. When the footsteps became faint, the pair of trespassers emerged from their refuges to sleuth through more of the jumbled papers that littered the workbenches. Braxton picked up a small journal from the table that had a title scribbled across the front in ink: *Reflections of Transcending Human Mortality.* The journal had logs of various dates that seemed to be in the early days of Cliff's discovery of the serum. Handwriting within the journal became less legible and neat towards the end and many of the pages were stained with ink blots and droplets of purple liquid. The entry that Braxton flipped to was one of great intrigue.

This particular page was near the end of the collection and featured swaths of unintelligible writing. Some phrases and sentences could be interpreted as the author seemed to be losing their train of thought and wits as his pen crossed the parchment. One sentence talked about Cliff beginning to get headaches and experience moments of vacancy in his mind that he concluded were seizures. A later scribbling mentioned that Cliff had some sort of reaction to a golden ring he'd been wearing earlier in the afternoon. Braxton turned the page and found a singular sentence staring back at him. The line read: "Nothing gold can stay, and only gold can abbreviate this eternal blight that ails me."

Cliff had found out that what had once been a grand idea of infinite life was now a hell of endless pain. He'd found the lethal antidote to his predicament but failed to bring himself to use it. Whether madness or hesitance overtook the sorry individual, Cliff was now in a prison he'd fabricated to liberate himself from the firm grasp of death. That fountain of youth had backfired and now spewed its fiery, boiling waters of wrath onto its baffled creator. Braxton pitied the poor fellow.

Gold was something that Braxton didn't imagine would be too onerous to find in the lavishly decorated manor. After telling Albus of his findings, the pair slowly ascended the stairs out of the laboratory. Dust particles had begun to dance in the air of the dimly lit study that had been deserted for some time but now found itself disturbed by a traveler, a writer, and a ghastly creature. The pair trod lightly through the halls until they came to the entrance of the grand mansion. Braxton went to try to open the door to give the men a means of escape before they plotted their scheme. Both of the brass knobs that had functioned to unlock and open the door had been busted off, leaving the door permanently sealed. As Albus took in the paintings that hung on the papered walls, Braxton examined the room and soon found his weapon of choice, a gold-plated chandelier that hung above their heads. This luxurious contraption of candles and gilded arms was anchored by a singular sturdy rope that ran to a balcony that overlooked the entry. Braxton was no interior decorator or chandelier snob, but he imagined that the ornamental prongs on the bottom of the fixture could do some damage.

Albus went to look for the stairs to the indoor balcony while Braxton went to seek out Cliff. Braxton walked through a pair of double doors that led to a kitchen that was a grotesque sight. Someone had begun butchering a cow in the room, but apparently got distracted and never returned. A hearty leg of beef that was now infested with flies still dangled from a meat hook. A bloody cleaver still sat wedged in a wooden cutting board. As he rounded a counter, Braxton got an introduction to the chef who lay limply on the tile floor. A syringe jutted from the man's chest where his heart once beat. The man's face was pale and his veins had become a deep purple. It would appear that this man was the first test subject of Cliff's serum. Cliff definitely was not a man of medicine for his patient looked long past help.

Braxton discarded the gruesome scene from his mind and continued down a hallway towards the back right portion of the mansion. Cliff Straus sat in an armchair by the fireplace that was faintly burning with just its embers left. In his hand, Cliff held a small portrait. This living space was dominated by the presence of family portraits and photographs that Cliff had accumulated to remind himself of what once was and would never be again. Braxton assumed the photo in the creature's deformed hand was a sacred family photo that Cliff clung to. A glimpse of humanity still seemed to be lingering behind the bloodshot eyes of the beast.

Braxton was so infatuated and intrigued by the room that he forgot he was standing in the middle of the hall, in plain view of Cliff. The slight remains of humanity vanished from the creature's eyes as it set the framed picture down and reached for its cane. A jolt of panic flowed through Braxton as the shock one receives from touching a hot stove. This jolt reminded Braxton that he was very much alive and in danger of not being much longer. The velvet rug slipped from under Braxton's feet as he scrambled to make his way back toward the disaster of a kitchen.

Muffled snarls and the thumping of the beast's cane ensured that Braxton was indeed being pursued. Braxton made his way out of the fly sanctuary of a kitchen as he heard Cliff come staggering through the doors on the other side of the kitchen. The entrance was in sight and Albus was nowhere to be seen which was actually not a bad sign. As the beast emerged from the kitchen, Braxton caught sight of Albus standing ready at the balustrade, rope in hand. Braxton lured the beast along until he stood beneath the chandelier. Without hesitation, Albus released the rope and the raucous of glass breaking and metal clattering made it seem as if a thousand servants had dropped metal trays that were piled high with champagne flutes simultaneously onto the hardwood floor. As the dust settled and the damage was done, Braxton looked to see if the chandelier had served its purpose. To his surprise, the creature that had once been pursuing Braxton was nowhere to be found. From under the rubble and twisted metal, Braxton heard a groan and saw the aged hand of a man. The hand removed a piece of the chandelier and revealed the face of a weathered man who had dark circles beneath his eyes and looked to be in his mid-sixties. It looked as if the chandelier had now pierced the man as much as it had pinned him to the floor. The tattered green suit didn't look much better, and Braxton noticed where the chandelier had actually punctured through the suit and into Cliff's skin. His right shoulder had a prong dug into it. The confined man looked up at Braxton who still wasn't quite sure if the chandelier had landed on him or Cliff. If Braxton didn't know any better, he'd say that Cliff was the luckiest man alive. Braxton's moment of awe was interrupted as the older gentleman who didn't look quite comfortable between the hardwood floor and the metal light fixture that held him down asked, "Would you mind getting this blasted thing off me? Us old timers don't do well on the floor."

Without a word, Braxton flipped the remains of the chandelier off of the man and helped him to his feet. The prong that had stuck Cliff had seemingly not punctured too deep into his back, but it didn't prevent the man from moaning and groaning as blood began to seep from the wound. Braxton got Cliff situated in a small chair as Albus made his way down from the balcony. Using a torn piece of the suit and a bit of ingenuity, Braxton fashioned a bandage for the old man. The old man let out a sigh as he took in his surroundings and the two men who were for some odd reason prying him out from under a chandelier in his entryway. Cliff remembered much of everything leading up to his failed experiment. He supposed that he owed the two men before him an explanation. Braxton and Albus both shifted their attention toward the man as he began his story, "So I suppose you both know my little secret…."

Chapter Twenty-Four
Reflections of the Regretful

Cliff Straus explained much of what Albus and Braxton had already found out for themselves. As the man sat in the shreds of his suit and dignity, Cliff seemed to sink deeper into remorse for his actions. After a brief debrief of Cliff's final memories prior to his unfortunate episode of self-degradation at the hands of his own creation, the three men went and found a space where they could all sit and take in their own thoughts. They settled upon a small cards table in the balcony where Albus had been positioned to drop a chandelier upon their newfound acquaintance. Cliff lit up a pipe with a stray match from the table and began smoking the pipe's remaining contents as if he'd just set it down a minute ago.

The table was cluttered with a deck of playing cards that had been scattered across the wooden surface as well as an ashtray and a few glasses that had been purged of their contents by a group of parched gamblers who had long since abandoned the table. Cliff continued his story comprised of fond recollections, "My parents used to have banquets and festivities here all the time to the point where I would awake each day to a new gathering or reason to celebrate. The glamor of my old life only began to fade when my parents' health began to decline. My father was due to pay for all the cigars and bourbon he consumed while my mother was taxed for all the cigarettes she used to put up with my father. In the end, my father would die the fall before my mother would that winter. That particular winter was exceptionally cold as I found myself trying to pick up the pieces of what had once been a life of indulgence and revelry. The parties and balls carried on for a while as I put on a false smile and laughed off the grief that now weighed upon my chest. After a few months of this charade, I began to become paranoid of death and sought out a way to negate the humanity I had been burdened with. I began teaching as a professor over at

Helmston University to help fund my research and gather materials. Sitting here now, I realize that what I once perceived as a burden is now a blessing. I do not wish to wallow in my pity and sorrow, for I've come to the epiphany that life is much more than just breathing and going through the motions. My parents lived a hundred lifetimes in the enjoyment and happiness they reaped from their lives while I foolishly opted to artificially stimulate that irreplicable phenomenon. What I experienced when I was corrupted by that serum was merely existing and hardly even that."

Braxton and Albus both looked at each other realizing that the man before them was shattered. He was mere pieces and scraps of what he could've been and more than likely wished he could be. There was still life after his mistakes, and Cliff seemed to be turning a corner toward reclaiming his fate. It is not our faults or errant deeds that define us, but rather, it's our responses and ensuing actions that truly define our character.

As Cliff came to terms with his imperfections and regrets, Albus and Braxton seemed to take a look at themselves in the cracked mirror of self-reflection that Cliff had just stepped away from. Braxton questioned whether he was truly living the way he desired in the whirlwind of adventures and new experiences he'd been swept up in. His perception of himself and this journey had become greatly reconfigured and altered in a way that Braxton deemed somewhat positive. He'd not set out to challenge some great aristocrat such as Pierce Wallace, but he'd found himself toe to toe with the polished man. There was no intention of Braxton getting anyone harmed or killed in the process of his mission, yet the blood of many seemed to have stained his coattails. Braxton had never imagined that what started as a modest quest for self-fulfillment would bloom into a twisted and gnarled network of tragedies and wonders that now seemed inexplicable. The man who stared back at Braxton through his consciousness was not the same as he'd been a matter of weeks ago.

The three men eventually set aside their mental tribulations and got back to the more pressing matters at hand. Cliff still had the key attached to a metal ring that hung from his belt which had surprisingly not been too badly damaged. Cliff brought the conversation back to life, "So, what brings you two to the dismal remains of Straus Manor?"

Albus sheepishly looked to Braxton for an answer as Albus preferred to keep his less-than-admirable actions to himself. Braxton responded to the question, "I'm here in search of a piece of the Knight's Crest. I'm assuming that you know what I speak of."

Cliff shifted in his chair and looked Braxton dead in the eye, "Well, that certainly switches the topic to another miserable subject. You've saved me from my own peril, so I could help you plunge deeper into your own. Interesting choice. If it is really what you want, here you go. This key will unlock the safe located in the upstairs bedroom in the East Wing. What about you now? Why are you here?" Albus fell under the gaze of Cliff.

Albus gave his questionable reason, "I'm just a nomadic writer who was looking for my next inspiration. I suppose when I heard about some strange creature here in Ramstead it piqued my interest. I apologize for my intrusion."

Cliff assessed the man across from him who had trespassed into his home. He wasn't necessarily angry as much as he was a bit intrigued. *What had he seen, and had he documented everything?* "I take no offense to human curiosity, but did you end up writing anything about my serum or the monster you observed?"

"I did, yes. Several pages as a matter of fact."

"Well, that's brilliant. Can I purchase them from you to add to my own research? I'm sure that the university will appreciate a complete report of the findings of my experiment. It might just be time for me to come out of my premature retirement and teach once more."

Albus made a deal with Cliff, "If you'll grant me the proper credit and could possibly put in a good word for me at Helmston then I'd be more than happy to. I think I might try my hand at inspiring some young literary minds."

"You've got a deal. I can certainly do that. What's your name, sir?"

"Albus. Albus Weatherly."

"Well, Albus, I invite you to accompany me to Helmston and we'll get you sorted there. As for your friend, he can do as he pleases."

Braxton was impressed that the pair of unlikely friends had hit it off so well. He left the pair of intellectual minds alone and dismissed himself from the table, thanking Cliff for the key. The hall that Braxton had walked through once before now had a faint trail of

126

purple droplets lining the runners. He briskly walked through the kitchen until he reached the study where he had first come face to face with Cliff. The room stood still as the embers flickered in the fireplace and a spider went about weaving its web in a dusty corner. In the middle of the room, the chair that Cliff had sat on was deeply stained with the serum, and a small picture frame lay where Cliff had discarded it in his pursuit of Braxton.

Braxton picked up the small frame to see a trio of three smiling people standing in front of the gates to Straus Manor. The slender woman on the left and the stocky man on the right seemed to be Cliff's parents. A youthful man with a lock of brown hair stood between the two with a half-moon grin on his face and his arms over the shoulders of his mom and dad. These people no longer wandered these halls, for two were gone with the wind and the young man was no longer the same. Time had passed and all that remained was the memories and shreds of Cliff's younger days. Braxton set the picture down and proceeded upstairs. Upon entering the bedroom, Braxton was bewildered.

A bed sat against the main wall with its linens and pillows all neatly in place. More pictures stood on the nightstand and across the walls showing scenic sights and family photos that Cliff had undoubtedly spent much time reminiscing over. The air in the room was stuffy as the windows had not been opened in some time. Braxton looked around the room for the safe and found that one of the nightstands had one built into it. The key turned smoothly in the lock and a couple of clicks could be heard from the locking mechanism. Braxton pulled the door handle and the door opened with a creak. The first part of the journey was complete.

Chapter Twenty-Five
Family Ties and a Web of Lies

Pierce Wallace found himself facing a wall both metaphorically and literally. His feet were set on his desk as he looked at one of the walls in his office. He had five days to pay his debts or he'd have to pay in a far less favorable way. At worst, Pierce planned to skip town and hide out from the political lackeys that the Council of the Great Expanse would send after him. Braxton was another matter that Pierce had found out would be harder to address than anticipated. Concerns about his brother's whereabouts also plagued the aristocrat's mind, for he had learned of his brother's escape from a letter left on his desk when he returned from his little get-together with Braxton. The odd part was that James had signed the letter himself and meddled with several of Pierce's possessions within his mansion. As Pierce leaned back further in his chair, he found another gift from his brother.

The back of the chair folded backward too far, dumping Pierce out of the chair and onto the mahogany floors of his own office. Two screws sat innocently on the floor where James had undoubtedly placed them after he removed them from the back of Pierce's chair. This show of brotherly love was becoming too common for Pierce who had discovered several of James's clever tricks and riggings. This family tie was going to drive Pierce mad or be the knot in the noose that would be his demise. A man couldn't even think about his own devious plans without having his older brother mess with him. Pierce peeled himself off the floor and dusted his shirt off before putting his chair back together.

When he was able to safely sit in his chair, Pierce ran through his plan in his head. He'd lead his remaining guards and servants along with him to intercept Braxton at Wanderer's Keep. The number of guards and servants at the mansion was beginning to dwindle as paychecks failed to arrive and others were given empty promises. One problem irked Pierce more than any other though. He had looked at the map of the Great Expanse on his wall all day and couldn't find anywhere named anything close to Wanderer's Keep. Even rummaging through old maps from centuries ago yielded nothing for the desperate man. He was stumped.

Pierce knew he wouldn't be able to simply follow Braxton to the keep as he had already caught onto Asmodeus watching over his travels. Asmodeus had been a wild card from the start as he wasn't somebody that Pierce trusted entirely. He'd gained a smidgen of intel from the spy and nothing more. Pierce's mind began to race with theories of the unknown. *James might've figured out where the fabled location of the keep and kept it to himself after all these years or perhaps he had told Braxton. Or perhaps Braxton had found out by some other means and had kept it under wraps so that no prying ears would ever know what he knew. Everyone had their hands of cards and it was coming time to show them. It was too late to fold and too early to declare a winner. All would be settled in Wanderer's Keep, wherever that was.*

Pierce grabbed a globe from a nearby shelf and spun it to get a good look at the Great Expanse. All the cities were labeled and even a few castles, which no longer were quite as formidable as they once were, had been denoted on the sphere. *Was this some sort of cruel riddle formulated to baffle the simple-minded or was the whole tale of the Book of Knowledge some kind of myth that had been kept alive for too long? It was out there. It had to be.*

After putting the globe back on the shelf, Pierce sat and looked around his room further for any clues that his father may have left him. His dad was one of the people who had allegedly been involved in the creation of the *Book of Knowledge*. The room which was cluttered with every trinket and book imaginable seemed empty to the man who was scouring for obvious clues that he hoped would jump off the shelves and walls at him. Pierce was beginning to believe that his father had played one last trick on his ungrateful son, but then he spotted something. A small framed picture of his parents sat smiling back at him from a distant shelf. It had been one of the few items that Pierce had directly inherited from the remains of his father's estate. Being reminded of his father was a bittersweet memory, for his father had been such a great man who had truly made a difference and here Pierce sat in his house of cards that was about to be blown over. James had always been compared to their father more than Pierce, for James was the golden child who could do no wrong while Pierce could do no right. Pierce couldn't bring himself to hate James, but their youthful years had certainly driven a wedge between the two. If he could do it all over again, Pierce knew he would end up exactly in the same spot as he lingered now. Pierce was fated to harness the *Book of Knowledge* and take rightful control of the Great Expanse. The pathetic pawns who stood in his way would seem like minor inconveniences when he was finished.

All that was left was to complete the last leg of the race that would bring all parties to Wanderer's Keep. Pierce just had to find out how to get there. He gazed to the large map that dominated the eastern wall of his office. Only upon his second viewing of the map did he notice something peculiar. There was a strange marking over an island off the western coast of the Great Expanse. A small fort called Herald's Stronghold was situated on the coast nearest to the island. Pierce got up from his chair and walked closer to the map. The marking was a "J" and a "W" which undoubtedly signified that his brother was responsible for the mark. The island was otherwise untouched and unmarked as it seemed like another insignificant blip in the middle of the sea. *Had his brother actually given him a clue or had he just set up one grand ruse to truly get a good laugh?*

It was all Pierce had and he was inclined to work with what he had been given. His brother did mention that he would see Pierce soon in the last place he'd expected. *Perhaps his brother was camped out on this island awaiting Pierce to arrive only to snicker at how gullible he'd been. Or maybe James was playing the game and baiting both Pierce and Braxton into bringing all the pieces to this random remote island to have the Book of Knowledge for himself?*

Nothing was for certain with this game that had developed facets that none of the players could've possibly guessed. Pierce removed the piece of the Knight's Crest from his pocket and analyzed its glossy surface. It seemed to taunt him with its partialness that beckoned the holder to find the other puzzle pieces. Braxton had done the dirty work and retrieved all the pieces from their resting places. All that was left to do was to take the pieces from him and complete the Knight's Crest which would enable him to claim the *Book of Knowledge.* Pierce loved a long con, but he became worried that he was about to become snared in his own intricate contraption.

This lengthy plan had become warped and improvised as pieces of Pierce's cobbled-together plan began to disappear or become a victim of the game. Kingston Devalve had initially been the person that Pierce had employed to seek out the Knight's Crest, but he had been crushed by the rolling stone that was Braxton Sterns. Pierce knew he would've been able to get what he wanted from the foolish gambler, but Braxton was a loose end that had begun to unravel Pierce's entire tapestry of planning. If this continued, Pierce would be sitting on a pile of frizzled strings and Braxton would have the *Book of Knowledge* at his disposal. It was time to prune the string.

Pierce grabbed a revolver from a desk drawer and tucked the piece of the Knight's Crest back into his coat. He gathered a few men from the halls, including Lucas, and got a fleet of wagons ready to embark on the journey. Wagons were hitched and supplies were loaded as men meandered through the wagon garages. Banners were draped and swords were polished as the miserable men of Pierce Wallace awaited the dreaded field trip that sat in front of them. Horses whinnied as they were hooked to wagons as Pierce's last staff commander barked orders across the building. Lucas sat shining the buttons on his uniform as the revolver that was at his waist felt especially heavy this particular afternoon. He secretly hoped that Braxton would win this mad dash and prevent Pierce from accomplishing his conceited goals. That remained the only reason that Lucas had remained in service to Pierce was to have the chance to aid Braxton when it mattered most, for Lucas had a strange feeling about Braxton. He seemed to exude positive intentions and level-headedness in each breath he took, and it gave Lucas hope that the Great Expanse was not devoid of good people. Working under Pierce Wallace had the negative aspect of gradually losing the human sense of faith in the world around him. Pierce was a wolf in sheep's clothing that was about to pounce upon what he perceived as a vulnerable member of the flock. As the last of the crates of supplies were loaded, everyone boarded their mounts and wagons to settle in for what lay ahead. The game board was set and the clock was ticking. All that was left was to play the game.

Chapter Twenty-Six
The Falling of the Rain

Rain softly pattered against the cloth covering of Braxton's wagon. Braxton sat in the driver's seat of the wagon, clothes soaked and eyes wandering across the dampened scenery. He possessed not a single care in the world, yet he also had all the weight of the world upon his shoulders. Ignorant bliss would be what most would call it, but Braxton preferred to call it contentment amidst stress. The man was aware of his situation and had already calculated his next move, so all that was left to do was enjoy the ride back to Longwood. Droplets of rain ran down the man's face as he steadily held the reins to keep the wagon on track. Braxton had begun this endeavor in a rushed frenzy to find what he was looking for, but now he was satisfied to just live for tomorrow and his next destination.

The path was beginning to become mud, as the rain had not ceased for some time now. What once had been a hardened culmination of gravel and dirt had become a soup of loose rocks and sloshing muck. Galileo didn't seem to mind too much that his underbelly had become caked in dried silt that had been flung up by his hooves. The pines of Ramstead filled the air with a nostalgic aroma of pine needles and sap that reminded Braxton of his youthful days spent wandering the evergreen forests with his friends looking for caves and other childhood novelties. Braxton wished he could return to his innocent days of boyhood before adulthood had complicated his life.

Unfortunately, there was only here and now for Braxton to enjoy as the rain continued to fall from the cloudy heavens. He was in no hurry to outrun the rain as it seemed that every inch of the sky had become blanketed in dark gray clouds. Much like his fate, the rain was inevitable, so he might as well welcome it and make the best of it. As he left the pines of Ramstead behind, Braxton once again found himself in the endless rolling hills that would eventually bring him to Longwood. The sheep in the meadows cowered beneath the branches of the few oak trees that offered their protection from the rain. Sparsely adorned with leaves, the branches of the oaks seemed to be doing little to prevent the sheep and their wool from becoming victims of the rain. The wooly coats that had once been fluffy blankets to shield them from the cold now weighed them down and contributed to the cause of their incessant shivering.

Braxton was beginning to feel the cold himself as his nose began to run. Wiping his nose with a soaked handkerchief was not the most pleasant experience, but it sufficed. Comfort was not something that Braxton could afford with his empty pockets and idle hands that still clutched the leather reins. Nature was not the most welcoming host, but it was an improvement to lurking around the halls of a dilapidated mansion owned by a disfigured monstrosity. Whichever way the wind blew at this point, Braxton was willing to ride it out.

With four of the five fragments of the Knight's Crest, Braxton was a small leap from achieving his overarching goal. All that stood in his way was this spurt of rain, Pierce Wallace, and a few more miles of trail to reach Wanderer's Keep. Wanderer's Keep was something that Braxton had tucked into his mind and never reopened, but he now realized that he knew nothing of such a place or where to find it. Another challenge appeared before Braxton, but he had a feeling it would work itself out. Perhaps his father knew about the location or the pieces formed some kind of map that would guide him there.

Braxton was focused on what lay ahead of him and nothing more for the moment. He had to reach Longwood before anything else could be done. The wooden wagon wheels tore through the muddy trail as it passed over the hills. Unscrewing the flask he'd procured from his vest pocket, he took a few sips of his favorite scotch that briefly warmed the damp traveler. The scotch reminded Braxton that there was still something other than dreary rain and struggle before him. There was indeed some satisfaction and contentment to be reaped from his life still even if he didn't have the *Book of Knowledge*. As his spirits brightened and his flask became a bit more empty, Longwood came into view on the horizon.

Rain dripped from rooftops and gushed from the gutter systems that line the roofs of the homes of Longwood. The streets were empty aside from a couple of wagons that had been left to the elements and a burly man in a pair of overalls who sat outside of a pub smoking a cigarette. Braxton passed by unlit shop windows and locked doors on his way to his parents. When he turned onto his parents' street, he saw something, or rather someone, peculiar sitting on their front porch.

James Wallace had been quite busy since leaving Holcomb Penitentiary, and he'd finally settled down to smoke a cigar on Braxton's parents' front porch. He'd left some tidings for his brother, Pierce, in his mansion which he was surely discovering the hard way. James had also given his brother the location of Wanderer's Keep to lure him away from his cowardly tactics. The strategy had worked as James had received news of Pierce's departure earlier in the day from an insider within Pierce's staff. Prior to Braxton's visit to him at the Holcomb Penitentiary, James had wanted to distance himself from anything to do with the Knights of Dark and the *Book of Knowledge*. Braxton's visit had awakened a fear within James that his brother might actually get what he wanted out of his plans. If Pierce achieved what he wanted, he'd overturn the entirety of the order of the Great Expanse and completely corrupt a system he'd already been polluting for quite some time. No man should be allowed to wield that kind of power, especially a maddened aristocrat of the likes of Pierce. James knew he'd have to aid Braxton in getting the book for himself in order to entertain the chance of destroying it for good. His father had issued a warning upon his deathbed that the book would be the undoing of everything and everyone, and no one was fit to possess such a powerful item. James had ignored his father's caution until he realized that a plot was in the works for his own brother to retrieve the book from its resting place. All the pieces of the Knight's Crest had been uncovered and the game was now on partly due to James's foolishness. He'd given Braxton his piece out of hope that Braxton would fail and find a new hiding place for the pieces. Braxton had succeeded, therefore, everything went wrong.

Braxton's wagon came to a halt in front of his parent's house as James pulled the cigar from between his lips and set it in the ashtray that Braxton's dad had set there. James greeted the person whose parents' porch he was occupying, "Good afternoon, Braxton. I warned you that we would cross paths again. We have much to discuss."

A look between confusion and intrigue swept across Braxton's face as he took in the loafer at his parents' doorstep. Braxton addressed the familiar stranger, "I thought you were content in your homely cell over in Holcomb Penitentiary, and how did you find my parents' house?"

"Well, to answer your second question, it's a small world out there. On the note of your first question, you and I are both in great peril, for which I have a proposal to help us clean up the mess we've found ourselves wrapped up in."

Braxton took a seat in the rocking chair next to James and addressed the man, "I'm aware that your brother still has the last piece, but what else is there aside from the obvious at hand?"

"There are many facets of this situation we have become ensnared in that you and most likely I won't understand ever. What I do know is that Pierce knows you have the rest of the pieces and he knows the whereabouts of Wanderer's Keep, partially because I told him where it was."

"So, you messed up and need my cooperation to lessen the blow? That's what I'm getting from this."

"Not quite, but sure. We have the upper hand here, but I fear that by some misguided fortune, my brother has begun to turn the tables on me and you. I'll admit that I've had a hand in worsening our predicament, but I believe that I've devised a plan to finally end this catch twenty-two that we find ourselves locked into. From what I know, Pierce is armed and bringing a crew of men to the island to await your arrival. My plan involves giving my brother exactly what he wants. We make an agreement with him to unlock the vault and retrieve the book as long as you are given the first opportunity to use it. You will then be faced with a decision as to whether you are to keep the book for yourself or vanquish the evils that lurk within the book by destroying it."

Braxton thought about James's plan and just how much risk it possessed. After thinking about it for a brief moment, Braxton posed one of the looming questions he had, "Can the book even be destroyed? That seems like a solution that would've been executed long ago if it was possible."

"I believe that it is not possible to destroy the book, but it can be defaced beyond recognition. It's like tarnishing the finest art piece to ever grace the halls of any museum, but our art piece in this case is a ticking time bomb that is about to go off in all our hands."

It was intriguing to humor the fact that a tall glass of grape juice could be the Achilles heel of one of the greatest works of all time. A messy toddler could be this all-powerful book's worst nightmare. Braxton issued one more question for James, "Well, if that fails, do you have a backup plan or are we riding on being able to vandalize one of the most formidable books to ever plague the face of the planet?"

"The backup plan is that we simply have to kill Pierce. Although completely immoral, the alternative to letting him get his scheming hands on this book would be bad for all parties present. I could afford to trim my family tree a little if it helps save everyone from his boundless wrath."

Braxton realized the gravity of his situation at this point. He was faced with a choice to attempt to end the issue for good or postpone the inevitable by beginning the largest game of chicken the world had ever seen. The odds of survival were better if Braxton simply went head to head with Pierce rather than waiting for mercenaries to be dispatched to come after him. In the back of his mind, Braxton still pocketed the idea of somehow keeping the book for himself. Sitting on his parent's front porch, Braxton devised a plan to make sure that he left Wanderer's Keep with the *Book of Knowledge*.

James interrupted his moment of contemplation, "So, are you willing to go forward with this? I could completely understand if you would like to avoid the threat altogether."

"No, no. I say we end this. I'll go through with it, but I just need a little time to gather some supplies and see if I can convince another friend of mine to accompany us. One thing before I fully agree to this, where is Wanderer's Keep and why do you know where it is?"

"Wanderer's Keep is a small island off the coast from a fort by the name of Herald's Stronghold. The way that I found out the location of this place is that I've come into contact with the man who claims to inhabit the keep above the vault. He's a wandering scholar who I met when we were both much younger. He has many aliases, but his true name is Rowan Alder. I first encountered him when he was looking for a place to stay when I lived in Havenstein for a little while. In exchange for a place to stay, Rowan gave me my piece of the Knight's Crest and told me about Wanderer's Keep. He said that what he was telling me would come in handy down the road, but I didn't foresee myself ending up in this position."

Braxton paused for a moment before responding, "Well, we don't pick the hands we're dealt in life, so we might as well make the best of them."

James replied, "I suppose that is so. I'll meet you in Havenstein at the Watchman's Inn near the east side of town tomorrow morning. Till then my friend."

After reclaiming his cigar, James got up from his chair and made his way down the street toward the outskirts of Longwood.

The terms were set and the air was cleared. The rain ceased, yet gray clouds still hung in the sky. The contest for the *Book of Knowledge* was beginning to veer toward an end. The pieces were beginning to fall into place.

Chapter Twenty-Seven
The Means to the End

Braxton sat on the front porch for a while longer, watching as the dull clouds shifted overhead. After a period of contemplation and cloud gazing, he went inside to reclaim his pieces and receive advice from his father. His mother stood over a counter in the kitchen, slicing vegetables for the large pot of soup that sat on the stove. The soup filled the house with the aroma of its chicken broth and assorted greens that reminded Braxton of his younger days having the flu with the only relief he could find being his mother's homemade chicken noodle soup. He was home once again.

Patrick Sterns sat in his small office scribbling on a form with a fountain pen. The office was cluttered with clocks, framed pictures, and other trinkets that fascinated him. Under the desk, a sleek black dial jutted out that guarded the contents of the safe. Patrick looked up from his papers to address his visitor. "Good afternoon, Braxton. How did you find things over in Ramstead at the Starus Manor?"

"Well, it's quite the long story that I'll have to save for another rainy day as I don't have much time. Let's just say it wasn't exactly glamorous, but I did get the fourth piece of the Knight's Crest. I've got to pick up my other three fragments and meet someone over in Havenstein tomorrow to finally bring this endeavor to a close."

"It seems like you've got everything figured out, Braxton. Just make sure this is what you truly want, for you are about to breach the threshold of irreversible action. I wouldn't want you to doubt yourself if you're confident in what you're doing, but I do want to bring the voice of reason upon your ears. Ensure that what you are about to become entangled in is truly just in your eyes, my boy. If you are certain and your conviction proceeds you, here are the fragments that you left with me within this burlap sack."

The fabric bag was not the vessel that Braxton envisioned carrying some of the most valuable items in the Great Expanse in.

With its scratchy and rough surface, the sack was nothing of much note to anyone who was not aware of its contents. It was the perfect, deceptive measure needed to deter the grubby, prying hands of thieves and maddened aristocrats alike. Braxton procured the fourth piece from his jacket and literally and metaphorically put all his eggs in one burlap basket. If the ruse failed, it might cost him everything, but Braxton had much more than the fear of petty theft and deception weighing on him. Braxton replied to his father after setting the bag on the oak desk, "I'm quite positive that what I'm doing is right. I've had much time to think and ponder, but now the time has come to execute rather than fantasize and hope. I sincerely do appreciate your advice, dad, for without it, I don't know if I'd be sitting where I am."

Braxton's father attempted to conceal the smile that was beginning to tug at the corners of his mouth. The grin spread despite his best efforts, and it seemed as if the man was proud of something his son had to say for once. Whatever coldness had covered his father's compassion and affection for years seemed to melt away for a moment before returning briskly to put the icy mask back into place. His father did truly possess expressions beyond cold stares and disturbed glares.

For the first time in decades, Braxton hugged his father. His father seemed stunned at the action, for it took him a moment to realize what was occurring and to return the favor to his son. After concluding the brief embrace, Braxton couldn't tell whether his father was paralyzed of shock or offended beyond words. He hoped for the first.

Oddly enough, Braxton's father was the first to breach the silence, "You should be going as it's getting quite late, my boy. Once you return from wherever you're off to now, we'll have to have a drink together and celebrate your success."

"I might have to take you up on that. Till I return then, I suppose. Goodbye, Dad."

Braxton picked up the bag containing the fragments of the Knight's Crest and made his way out of his parent's home before his mom could catch wind of his departure. As much as he'd like to tuck into a bowl of his mother's soup and humor her comments about his wrinkled shirt and messy hair, Braxton knew that time was of the essence. Braxton and Galileo soon found themselves back at their once familiar homestead that now seemed like more of a rest stop than their home. The sun sunk beneath the horizon as the moon began its slow ascent towards the darkening sky that was becoming dotted with small stars. Sleeping in his own bed was a peculiar phenomenon that was both odd and comforting at the same time. It was almost as if he'd forgotten what it felt like to not be sleeping in a wagon or under the scratchy linens of an inn. Braxton dozed off with ease as his body felt as if it may never want to get up from the silken sheets and cushy mattress.

When he awoke, Braxton was delighted to be in his own bedroom for once in the past few weeks. It was early in the morning as the bleak night was still fleeting from the sky, and the bright morning seeped in. For the first time in a while, Braxton put on a fresh set of clothes that weren't wrinkled and poorly folded in a suitcase. His forest green button-up was tucked into his black trousers that were secured around his waist by a black leather belt. His pair of brown oxfords seemed to shine on his feet as the morning sunlight poured through the windows of the cliffside cottage. After getting his hair orderly and belt straightened, he went upstairs to his study to grab one last item before departing. Braxton perused the shelves of his study for a particular object. He set his sights on a medium-sized book that had a black dust jacket wrapped around it. It seemed to be the perfect decoy that Braxton could pass off as the *Book of Knowledge*. The book's title had long faded off by time and dust as it had sat on the shelf for quite a while. Braxton tucked the book into the inside of the jacket he would be wearing to Wanderer's Keep.

Shortly after gathering his things and ensuring that the wagon was stocked with everything he'd need for the short journey, Braxton headed out towards Havenstein to meet James at the Watchman's Inn under the rays of the golden sun.

Chapter Twenty-Eight
Inns and Outsiders

T he Watchman's Inn was not much to behold. With its faded shutters and sun-baked brick walls, the building was firmly packed between Wexton's Jewelers and Johnston's Woodworking. On the small covered porch jutting from the front of the structure, James Wallace sat smoking a cigar and drinking a glass of orange juice. James was dressed in a brown jacket that overlapped his white undershirt and a pair of jeans. A leather suitcase sat by his feet.

The winter sun beat down on Braxton as if the very heavens were watching his every motion under the stellar spotlight, eagerly awaiting something exciting or tragic. Braxton sought shelter under the eaves of the porch as he approached James who shifted his gaze onto Braxton. James greeted his newfound corroborator, "Good morning, Braxton. Are you ready to change the fate of the world? I hope so, for we have quite the day ahead of us. I've received news that Pierce has reached Wanderer's Keep and is presumably awaiting your arrival. A surprising development has been made, as it would appear that many of Pierce's men deserted his sinking cause, leaving him with only a few servants and guards. Our odds look better and it would appear that violence may not be necessary in this situation, for our formidable obstacle appears to be dissolving before us in the seawater surrounding Wanderer's Keep."

"Seems like as ample a morning as any, James. I'm glad our odds are improving, for we're going to need all the help we can get to cut through your brother's lunacy. Who is this fabled informant that you possess? It won't do any good to keep this a secret any longer as all will surely be revealed by the time the sun sets on us tonight."

"Well, if you must know, the insider that I've befriended would be Asmodeus Grimes. A peculiar fellow with few allegiances he is. A perfect candidate for the spark that would help burn Pierce's kingdom of straw to the ground swiftly. An old family friend that has gotten wedged between two squabbling brothers and has finally seen the true colors of Pierce Wallace. He's currently camped out on a secluded seaboard overlooking the island of Wanderer's Keep. There is a rowboat that he's arranged for us to take from his campsite near the northern shore."

"I had a feeling that man had his hands in more than scenic paintings and traveling the countryside. At least we've got someone on our side besides ourselves."

James took a sip from his glass of juice and then added, "I believe we have everyone aside from Pierce and his followers behind us. They just don't know it yet. We're here to protect the common good, therefore, the common folk of every desolate village and urban sprawl is represented in our actions. Our hands are theirs and our voices speak for the general welfare in destroying the *Book of Knowledge*. We are not only executing our own wills but also that of every person who wishes to remain devoid of Pierce's maddened influence. I hope you understand the gravity of our undertaking, Braxton."

"I don't believe I ever will comprehend the grim results of failure, for I don't plan on failing and if I do then there will be no value in regret. This is one of the few times in my life that I believe failure is a possibility. Most other challenges merely offer the chance to make a mistake and learn from it rather than deciding the fate of the Great Expanse. We should probably be going if we'd like to make it to the shore by noon."

James got up from his seat and took his empty glass inside as Braxton stood alone on the deck. The winter snow had fully melted off, leaving a taste of warmer weather across the dry ground that had begun to thaw under the warm sunshine. A sole reminder of the winter season lingered in the barren tree branches that stretched towards the second and third stories of the buildings they guarded. The streets of Havenstein were quite deserted, as many had either arrived at their jobs by this hour or were still content at home. A few cafes were alive with groggy patrons who sipped from their coffees and teas to garner some form of energy for the day ahead. Most stores were not quite opened, yet as doors remained locked while storekeepers swept floors and straightened displays for the onslaught of customers this summerlike day would bring. All of these people were outsiders to a war that they were oblivious to. The events that would unfold meant everything and nothing to these people as they went about their day, tending to their pocketbooks and responsibilities.

The door to the inn came open as James emerged with his cigar clutched between his lips. As the door clicked shut, Braxton felt as if he had sealed his fate as the point of no return had been reached. The ground behind him seemed to vaporize as there was no direction but forwards. His convictions propelled him as the two men boarded the wagon and set off for the island of Wanderer's Keep. Galileo trotted on once more, unbothered by the presence of another piece of living cargo that he'd acquired somehow. This journey had granted Galileo an escape from the monotonous pastures of the homestead and allowed him to find purpose in toting around his adventurous owner who seemed to find his own delight in the long, winding trails.

While James continued to work on his cigar, Braxton remained behind the reins as the sky began to become clouded, stifling the unexpected yet welcomed burst of warm sunshine that had been pouring down all morning. Snow began to lightly fall from these clouds that had ushered in another reminder of the icy season. The trail continued on over hills and dales that brought Braxton and James closer to their destination. After about a mile of listening to the crunch and pop of gravel on the wooden wheels, James asked Braxton a question he was not prepared to answer, "How did we get here?"

Braxton took his eyes off the trail ahead for the first time since leaving Havenstein. This question had a simple answer that shielded the more complex reason from daylight. Braxton issued an answer that James took great interest in, "I believe I've gotten here out of my own curiosity and need for meaning to my life. You seem to be here to hinder your brother's malicious efforts to obtain the *Book of Knowledge*. I know that it is not as easy as that to paint a vivid picture of our motivation, but that is my perception of exactly how and most likely why we're here riding down this dusty trail."

"I suppose that's a fair and reasonable answer. All this commotion has me wondering about my own motivations to put down my brother's antics. The true question is: what is it all for? Am I merely settling a score with my younger brother or am I truly out for the common good? I'd like to think of my reasons as virtuous and benevolent, but I seem to be acting much on impulse and short term planning. It's a shame that it seems like this has devolved into some petty contest between two brothers who feel the need to alienate those around them with their problems and concerns. I'm glad that I've found someone who shares an interest in my objective, for I feel as though I've been dragging people along behind my own ambitions. Just know that if we never cross paths after this, you've earned my respect, Braxton."

Braxton looked at James in a new light of clarity and lucidity that showed just how much James cared and thought of his actions. He was no short-term planner or someone who operated on whims or fascinations. The man before him operated in the interest of everyone around him and used his clever wits to get what he feels he needs. Braxton transferred the reins into one of his hands and issued a response to James's profound reasoning, "I appreciate that. As someone who believes respect cannot be expected or bought, another man granting me the right to his illustrates that we've truly found an understanding of each other. We are all in need of meditation in cathedrals of our own which I believe we'll have plenty of time for after this whole charade ends. Until then, I'm glad I could be an outlet for your inner concern and worry, for what we are about to embark on is no small feat. May we strike true in our actions for the good of ourselves and everyone out there who we can spare from Pierce's wrath."

James pulled his cigar from his mouth and responded, "All that is left is to do what we feel is correct. There will be time for explanations and justifications later, but in order to achieve the outcome we desire, we must believe what we are doing is just. If we don't have faith in our own morality and stance, then who does? We are the pilots of our own wayward fate at this point, so we might as well make the best of it. Where we stand, we are not pieces on a checkers board anymore, but rather, we are the ones eye-to-eye with our common enemy, contemplating our next move to control the board. We have the upper hand. All we have to do is use it."

The ramparts and battlements of Herald's Stronghold came into view after about another hour of light snow and conversation. Cannons looked out over every wall awaiting the next foolish invader they would be able to turn to ash and dust. Men in silver helmets walked along the walls with spears and swords in hand and on their hips. Most didn't seem to pay the approaching wagon much mind, as it was no Trojan horse or intimidating war machine. The gray brick walls of the castle loomed over everything around it, including Braxton and James who now felt like ants approaching the house of a giant. After passing by the fort, the shores came into view with their sandy surfaces and wavering tides. A familiar wagon was parked on the beach with a small tent pitched beside it. A small skiff sat closer to the water as it awaited its next trip to sea. Asmodeus stood at an easel looking out to the keep that stood defiantly on a distant island. Even amidst the intricate life of spying and traveling all over the countryside, there was time for the man to get in a little painting to take the edge off of his chaotic schedule. Asmodeus's horse was tethered to a tree far from the shore as it pulled at the remaining grass that was beginning to be claimed by the grasp of winter.

Braxton's wagon rumbled down the rocky trail that led to the coarse sands of the beach. Asmodeus put down his palette and brush and walked back to his seaside campsite. After parking the wagon, James and Braxton collected supplies from the wagon and began walking towards the campsite as well. The time for planning and pondering was over. It was time to put the plan into motion.

Chapter Twenty-Nine
Hands of Greed and Fortune

A smodeus was unusually chipper for someone in the position that he currently found himself in, but it was reassuring for Braxton to know that someone had a brighter outlook on this situation. The worst possible outcomes of this dire circumstance seeped into Braxton's mind, reminding him that he was very much mortal, and in turn, still just as vulnerable as ever. Humanity still flowed through his veins and thus it could be stripped away with a single bullet from the unhinged man they were about to come face-to-face with. Pierce was capable of being reasonable at times, but Braxton feared that the man was running out of patience and time to humor being level-headed. Lurking in Braxton's mind, the idea of simply walking away from the whole ordeal and going into hiding seemed appealing; however, he knew he would just be kickstarting another game in which Pierce would hunt him down to the ends of the earth. It was coming time to end this debacle once and for all.

While Asmodeus slowly worked on getting the skiff to the water, James loaded a round of ammunition into his revolver that Braxton had been completely oblivious to since they'd left Havenstein. This was reality, and this was about to happen. Braxton had to find a mode to collect himself and recapture the calm and cool mindset that had gotten him this far.

After he finished loading the revolver, James tucked it into his belt and began helping Asmodeus move the boat and oars toward the water. Braxton still possessed his old revolver that had been loaded since his last neighborly chat with Pierce. With the burlap sack that held the pieces tied to his belt, he felt that he was finally prepared to end this prolonged contest for the *Book of Knowledge*. The last thing that Braxton wanted to be at this time was unprepared or vulnerable to anyone or anything.

As the skiff began to buck and bob in the shallow water, the three men boarded and Asmodeus and James picked up the oars to begin their voyage to Wanderer's Keep. The smell of seawater and the caw of the gulls overhead reminded Braxton of his time at sea with Captain Winthrop aboard his much more comfortable sailboat. The wooden benches in the boat creaked and rocked as the boat was tossed about by the waves. James and Asmodeus did their best to guide the boat through the restless waters that occasionally threw fistfuls of frigid ocean water into the faces of all members of the motley crew of sailors. Asmodeus handed Braxton a small spyglass from the pocket of his vest. Between rows, Asmodeus told Braxton, "See what Pierce has orchestrated at the island before we get too close. I'd rather not find out the hard way."

Braxton held the spyglass up to his eye, feeling the cold brass against his face. He adjusted himself until he was staring down the nearest shore of the island. A pair of rowboats sat unguarded and unmanned on the small beach. Following the trail from the beach to the keep, nothing seemed disturbed or out of place aside from a set of footprints in the sandy soil. It was too quiet, and Braxton had a bad feeling that it might not remain that way for much longer. The keep itself was a stout tower that had been heavily taxed by the sea as barnacles clung to the masonry on the lower levels and the bricks seemed pitted from their long-standing exposure to the salty winds of the gulf. A rusty cannon sat proudly on its balcony, overlooking the incoming sailors. Through one of the lower windows, Braxton could make out a pair of men seated at a table gesturing back and forth and exchanging playing cards. Pierce and his men apparently felt that now was a good time for a quick hand of five-card poker. Cigarette smoke seeped from an upper window. If he didn't know any better, Braxton would've thought he was approaching the most scenic pub in the entirety of the Great Expanse. However, Braxton knew that the hands that were dealing those cards were dishonest and the mouths that were smoking those cigars and cigarettes were crooked. Braxton had a premonition that five-card poker was not the only game that Pierce was playing here.

The small rowboat soon escaped its bombardment of the waves and seagull droppings to find itself beached next to a couple of other boats on the island of Wanderer's Keep. All the other boats were empty and the beach was silent except for the crash of waves on the shore. As the men unloaded themselves and their gear from the boat, Braxton spotted a familiar young man that peered at them from the balcony of the keep and then quickly retreated back inside the stone structure. Asmodeus and James jammed their oars into the yellow sand for the possibility that they may need to make a quick escape if events were to turn sour. This possibility was present in everyone's mind.

The men approached the keep cautiously, utilizing the presence of wilting greenery and barren trees to hide their ascent. An agent of fortune, a painter, and a former inmate walk into a keep. This would've been an amazing exposition to quite possibly the most intriguing joke ever told if Braxton wasn't living it. Any time for jokes seemed to be well behind them on the distant shore.

Pierce and a couple of familiar men sat at a table playing cards with one another. Next to Pierce, Lucas sat sheepishly as he glanced up from his hand to evaluate the visitors. Across the table from Lucas, the man who had given Braxton his carving of the owl in Merchant's Grove sat glaring daggers into the eyes of Pierce Wallace. Lastly, a man whom Braxton had never met or seen before was across from Pierce. The stranger had a pistol holstered to his belt and a sword on his opposite hip that hovered inches above the floor in its scabbard. Braxton presumed that the stranger was one of Pierce's last guards who apparently was the only man, besides Lucas, left on the aristocrat's payroll. As for the room, the place was filled with disorderly shelves full of old books, miscellaneous scientific instruments, and a few small paintings of the seaboard. A curved staircase led up to the balcony and second story of the keep that had been used to spot the landing party that now stood in the doorway of the keep. A locked door peered over the railing of the walkway, looking down towards the entrance. Pierce set down his cards and adjusted the cuff of his shirt where a spare ace of clubs was protruding from. After taking a sip from his glass of cognac, Pierce addressed his newfound company, "You're earlier than I expected, my friends. I assumed it would at least take a few days for you to gather the nerve and composure to follow your fates here." The aristocrat seemed to be staring down Braxton while he spoke as if they were the only two people left on the face of the earth. "The time for reason and negotiation still persists, so let us make use of this fleeting commodity."

James took the liberty of addressing his brother, "There is no need for negotiations of any sort, for you aren't in any position to bargain or deal. As much as I'd like to humor your foolish and selfish antics, I feel the time for comedy and tolerance has come to a close. Hand over your fragment and we might allow you to have one question for the book before we destroy the evil once and for all. If not, there are always other ways of getting what we want as I'm sure you're aware."

James and Pierce's guard reached towards their weapons on their belts as James glared at his estranged brother. Pierce didn't reach to his belt, but he rather seemed to be appraising the value of James's proposition. Braxton continued to analyze the room and took a moment to assess the man who he had previously met in Merchants Grove on his journey to find Merlin. Rowan Alder didn't seem to care for the situation as he looked uncomfortable and slightly aggravated at Pierce. The reasoning for this displeasure could've been the fact that his home had been invaded by a sleazy aristocrat and his pathetic legion or the steel shackle that kept him tethered to the bench that he was sitting upon. He'd become a prisoner of his own house, condemned to endure Pierce's flashy smile and unprincipled games. No matter what cards were in the man's hand, it was impossible for him to be a winner when he was being held hostage in his own study. Helpless and deprived of a reprieve, Rowan Alder had no choice but to sit and be a spectator of the grand show that Pierce was about to put on.

Braxton's focus shifted back to Pierce who had concluded his moment of contemplation and was now delivering his verdict. Pierce adjusted his collar and answered, "I'm not completely unreasonable, despite your preconceived notions, James. I'll agree to your deal as long as my one question is honored, regardless of your perception of it. I'd also like to add a condition that Braxton be allowed to determine the fate of the book and whether or not to truly destroy it. If he so chooses, he may keep the book for himself. That is my counter. Do with it what you will."

This stark change in direction intrigued and sent a wave of fear through James who didn't assume his brother would be one to negotiate. A catch had to be present in order for his brother to do anything of this nature. James also had to rely upon Braxton to make the correct decision and keep the book from falling into the hands of Pierce once it was in his possession. A medley of possibilities, both grim and reassuring, swirled through James's mind like wine in a

149

piece of stemware that James was about to taste. He was either about to be pleasantly surprised or sorely regretful.

James looked to Braxton to see if this proposition was agreeable to the man who had the biggest role to play in the grand mechanism that had gotten them to where they stood now. It took Braxton a moment to register what James had gotten him into. The entire fate of the *Book of Knowledge*, and quite possibly the world, rested on his shoulders under these circumstances. Pressure was an understatement of what Braxton felt. It felt as if every gram and ounce of matter in the world was crushing down on him as he stood on the stone floor of the keep. Every action that Braxton had done to get to this point stared him back in the face as the memories of meeting Merlin, Sir Edward Caldwell, Captain Winthrop, Albus Weatherly, and Cliff Straus surrounded him. The mental presence of all these people and everyone else he'd met seemed to be hanging on every word that raced through Braxton's mind. Braxton came up with a counter that he believed would close all the loopholes that Pierce eagerly awaited to be left open. Braxton issued his deal, "I'll grant you the one question and I'll take on the burden of felling the book. However, the answer to your question will be read out of the book by Asmodeus as to avoid any tampering or greed taking hold. That is the only offer that I'll allow you."

Pierce thought for a brief moment and then partially stunned everyone in the room with one word, "Deal."

James looked to Braxton with a look between concern and fear of what was to come, for Pierce seemed quite certain of his decision. All that was left was the consequence to the action. With all agreements made and arrangements complete, Pierce, James, Asmodeus, and Braxton ascended the stairs towards the locked door.

Chapter Thirty
The Difference Between Falling and Flying

A cool winter breeze blew through the second story of the keep as the four men reached the top of the stairs. All three of the men in Braxton's party seemed to shiver at this reminder of the winter season, but Pierce seemed unfazed by the shrill gust. Braxton supposed it was impossible for a man as cold as Pierce Wallace to become any more bitter from a simple inconvenience of nature. The door that stood between the men and the *Book of Knowledge* was an interesting feat of woodworking and carpentry that seemed to be the nicest fixture in the entire keep. Intricate carvings of different figures and scenes spread across the face of the door with a blank circle occupying the middle of the masterpiece. The time had come for the Knight's Crest to be whole once more.

James turned to Pierce, "It's time to uphold your end of the bargain. We'll take your piece and have Braxton put it in with all the others to ensure no foolish ideas are had."

Pierce sneered at his brother, "I know how a deal works, James. I've done my fair share of dealings and exchanges. One does not prosper in business unless they understand the basics of dealing. Here you are."

Pierce pulled the fifth piece of the Knight's Crest from his coat pocket and handed it to Braxton who couldn't tell if he should thank the aristocrat or take a couple of steps backward from him. Everything seemed to be moving too smoothly and honestly for Pierce not to have another trick up his sleeve aside from the ace of clubs that was still stowed away in his furled sleeve. Braxton gathered his four pieces from his burlap sack and put together the fragments that formed a medallion about the size of a small dinner plate. This ornate frisbee was now the most dangerous item in the entire Great Expanse, and Braxton was standing about five feet from the last man that anyone would ever trust near it. Asmodeus leaned on the railing of the walkway as Braxton admired the evil he clutched in his own two hands. Pierce seemed to smile as he watched Braxton place the Knight's Crest in the space on the door. The Knight's Crest snapped into place like a magnet latching on to a piece of steel. After a faint click of the crest settling in the door, every divot and rut in the door began to glow with a golden light that signified that Braxton had done something right. Braxton wasn't quite positive if what he was doing was necessarily "right" in this moment.

Anticipation built in the men as the intensity of the gilded light settled and became just another part of the art piece that was the door. The seal on the door gave way as the door became slightly ajar. Everything Braxton had labored and sacrificed for over the last month sat before him on a lectern that stood alone in the room that was little grander than a broom closet. Braxton examined the black leather cover of the book that was etched with a pair of crossed swords surrounded by a series of patterns and geometric shapes. This book had undoubtedly caused wars, murders, destruction, and fissures amongst friends and families. It was unbelievable that such an item sat before Braxton on the wooden lectern. James moved to block Pierce's view of the book as Asmodeus surrendered his spot against the railing to do the same.

When Braxton opened the book, pages began flipping without force and every possible question Braxton could possess flew by in an instant, from his mom's chicken noodle soup recipe to his dad's favorite color. The book landed on a page that was deeply intriguing to Braxton, for he knew exactly what question it answered. On the yellowed page, the words "Only you have the knowledge of that" appeared in silver ink. The pages ruffled again and the next set of words appeared, "Danger is imminent as long as I remain intact. I'd advise against doing what I believe you are about to do." Not even the book itself wanted to be here. That couldn't be a good sign.

Pierce finally spoke and demanded his question be answered. After Braxton had his fill of answered curiosities and backhanded responses from the book, he allowed Pierce his question. Asmodeus took Braxton's place in front of the lectern as Pierce asked, "Is there a way out of my current predicament?"

Pages ruffled as Asmodeus observed the words that appeared on the page as he channeled Pierce's question. The book's response was not satisfactory as Pierce seemed outraged and angered by the small book. Asmodeus read the following statement from the *Book of Knowledge,* "There is always a way to better oneself. However, in his case, I believe that he doesn't possess the means to do so. Money has been both his success and his downfall. Every creature that takes flight must hit the ground eventually. Pierce has indulged greatly in the ascent of his journey, but it is now time for the hubris-ridden man to partake in the descent."

Braxton translated that response to, "Pierce has made errors and choices in his life that not even a magical book could undo."

James held his brother back from the book as he madly scrambled to get a glimpse of the pages in hopes it would answer another question for his sorry self. Pierce's luck and fortune had run out and there was nothing that could revive the fading hopes that had died in the aristocrat's arms. Asmodeus allowed Braxton to grab the book from the lectern and tuck it away in his jacket. For something that held every piece of information known to man, the book was quite light, and felt like he was holding a small children's book rather than an all-knowing encyclopedia. Braxton now felt cheated that he had to tote around a bulky textbook in college rather than being graced with the portability of this great asset. Regardless, he set this societal injustice aside, for he could only handle one crisis at a time. Braxton looked to the stairwell to see Lucas peering around the corner of the railing, out of sight of Pierce's rage. Restraining the man seemed to be a tall order as Pierce wrestled and fought like a rabid animal rather than a polished philanthropist. To end the vicious struggle between James and his brother, Braxton decided it was time to execute his plan to put an "end" to the *Book of Knowledge.* Braxton knew that this book was far from invincible as the pages and cover had several signs of wear from sitting in the untouched closet for quite some time. None of this mattered as he had no true intentions of destroying the actual *Book of Knowledge.* Books were always susceptible to one form of destruction. This being that their paper interiors were quite flammable.

Asmodeus was helping contain Pierce as James was beginning to struggle to keep his brother at bay. Braxton noticed a matchbox in the back pocket of Asmodeus's trousers that he felt looked quite apt for burning one of the most coveted sources of information on the face of the planet. As the men staggered and stumbled back and forth, the matchbox that had been peeking out fell to the floor with a faint clack as the cardboard hit the wooden planks. After picking up the matches and retrieving his decoy book from his jacket, Braxton noticed that Pierce shifted his eyes to him as a match was lit on the railing. Pierce must've seen the flame of the match as his last ember of hope, for he made one final effort to lunge for the book. This attempt was quite successful as he barreled into Braxton who used every ounce of strength to keep his grip on the leather binding of the book and dropped the first match without igniting the book ablaze. The pair stumbled their way onto the balcony as Braxton struggled to light another match against a passing surface.

The book remained firmly in Braxton's grasp as he fought off the reckless attempts of Pierce to pry it from his hands through sheer maddened willpower. His advantage was fleeting, however, as Pierce was proving to be more of a formidable opponent than Braxton initially realized. As the pair twisted and turned, Braxton looked out over the north railing of the balcony to see the waves that stretched to the nearby shore. This sight gave Braxton an idea.

Many of Braxton's personal books had become ruined and stained in the past from his accidental spills of his nightly glasses of scotch and other liquids. Braxton was willing to wager that the seawater would do quite the number on the archaic book that the two men were scrapping over. With one assertive pull, Braxton loosened Pierce's grip on the book just enough to become in control of the object. Utilizing his fortunate window of opportunity, Braxton heaved the book over railing and into the jagged rocks and relentless waves below the cliff that the keep sat on. This would've been enough to deter further actions of determination from most as they watched what they had worked so hard for fly to its demise. Pierce was not quite that sensible.

Pierce dove towards the railing in a pathetic attempt to catch the book in flight before it became out of reach. The man must've underestimated his own maddened rush, for the shallow railing was not enough to prevent the man from falling off the balcony after the book. The selfish aristocrat had finally learned the true difference between what had once been a graceful flight of bliss that was now a helpless downward spiral of misfortune. He had discovered the sole difference between flying and falling: falling insinuates that one is hurtling toward something. Braxton supposed that the journey to the bottom of the cliff felt like effortless flying until Pierce inevitably hit the ground.

Lucas, Asmodeus, James, and Braxton cautiously gathered at the railing to process what they had just witnessed. The world had lost a man that carried with him many different titles and ties that were now vaporized in an instant. While the three had lost a common adversary, James in particular seemed the most conflicted as he seemed to be trying not to allow the tears to flow down his face while trying to retain his composure. The man had lost a brother at the end of the day. It seemed as if the weight of the world had shifted to his shoulders as James had lost the man he had known forever and had ventured through life with, for better or worse. Braxton also felt a mixture of emotions that unsettled him, for he had not expected to have to go to these great lengths to obtain what he wanted. He'd never fathomed that a man would have to die over such a cause that now seemed to have no value whatsoever. The book that remained in Braxton's pocket now felt quite heavier.

Asmodeus even seemed conflicted, as he had lost what at one point in his life had been a close companion before he became an adversary. Lucas seemed to be reflecting on his time with Pierce who he once perceived as a remorseless employer, but there was a newfound bond that had been unearthed. A strange relationship in which pleasantries and courtesies were rarely found. There was something to be said for a man who could make himself as wildly successful as Pierce and be as generous as he had been. None of that mattered much now as it had all been squandered away in the hasty pursuit of a grand solution to all the man's problems. Not even the *Book of Knowledge* would have the words to describe the waves of emotion that had overcome the men. The senseless end of any natural life was a true tragedy that cut through the tensions of every disagreement and difference to remind us that we are all merely human. Every man standing upon that balcony had made mistakes in their life, but one man had paid the ultimate price for his. A price that was more than any sum of gold or materialistic item could fulfill. The four men pulled themselves away from the railing and walked back inside the keep to collect their thoughts.

As Lucas delivered the news to Pierce's guard, Asmodeus unfastened the shackle from around Rowan's leg. The time for amends and reflection was upon them as what had been done had been done. Everyone sat in contemplation for a few moments in which few words were exchanged. After a brief deliberation, Asmodeus, James, and Braxton all decided that it would be best if they departed from the place to distance themselves from the trail of sorrow and loss that had tainted Wanderer's Keep. The three men boarded their skiff and headed for the mainland. Braxton and Asmodeus took the oars for this trip to allow James to focus on his thoughts. Voyaging back to the shore seemed to take an eternity longer than rowing out to the island initially had.

As the bow of the rowboat scraped against the sand, the men all filed out of the vessel and regrouped on the shore. Asmodeus was the first to leave as he promised to meet up with the two men again someday to catch up when the dust had settled. James seemed emotionally shattered after losing his brother as he walked up the hillside from the shore and propped himself against an oak tree that overlooked Wanderer's Keep which seemed like a small shadow in the distance. Braxton felt obligated to say something profound or thoughtful to ease the screaming pain that ailed James. However, before he could think of something meaningful, James spoke, "Just leave me be. I'll move on eventually, but for now, this is all I can bring myself to do. I'm sure we'll meet again, Braxton. For now, this is goodbye, my dear friend."

Braxton took this as his cue to honor the broken man's wishes and depart from the scene. After gathering his own composure and getting Galileo hitched to the wagon, Braxton began his journey back to the place where everything had begun.

Chapter Thirty-One
An End to a Beginning

In his study, Braxton sat in the midst of a gray fog that had overtaken his mind since his return from Wanderer's Keep. The people and places he'd been would occasionally emerge from this haze to remind Braxton that his coveted prize was not an individual effort to acquire. On his desk, the *Book of Knowledge* stared up at him from the clean surface that had been cleared off to make room for what Braxton had waited years to possess. An inkwell and a full glass of scotch were the only other items that occupied the desk aside from the book. The sporadic hoot of an owl and howling of a wolf was all that could be heard in the quiet night. While the ice cubes bobbed in his glass and his mind wandered, Braxton couldn't tell if he felt satisfied at finally achieving what he had long awaited or regretful at the price it had cost those around him. Selfishness was a term that Braxton refrained from branding himself with, as those who had paid for the book with their lives had done so primarily because of this destructive virtue. A constantly tilting scale of guilt and fulfillment weighed upon his mind as he remembered all the people he had helped and harmed to sit where he now sat. Two faces seemed to constantly plague his mind as he remembered one pair of people far more than any other, the Wallace brothers.

Pierce has been a well-respected philanthropist with a shaded personal life that had eluded the public eye for quite some time and would most likely never be discovered by anyone who didn't already uncover the secret. In the end, Pierce had thrown everything away to become something he was simply not worthy of: power. On the other hand, there was James who seemed to become engulfed in his brother's shadow when Pierce began his ascent to fame and fortune. James had lived modestly and became a threat to Pierce through his honest and righteous ploy to reveal his brother for his wrongful doings. Even after being imprisoned by his brother, James still wept over his brother's foolish sacrifice which showed that there was still something left to be salvaged between the two. James now sat with the shreds of the hand he was dealt in life, attempting to pick up the tatters of his father's fortune and dignity that Pierce had squandered so frivolously. Braxton had a feeling that all James needed was time to get back to where he wished to be.

That feeling was also one that Braxton felt for himself. Time would allow him to figure out what he wanted out of life. This is what Braxton figured the *Book of Knowledge* meant by its ambiguous answer to his burning question of his true purpose. What Braxton had once perceived as his true purpose now sat before him, mocking him with his success. Getting what he wanted only meant that Braxton had to find another something to look for out in the Great Expanse. Braxton thought of what he might start collecting or scouring the countryside for, but nothing appealed or came to him. An adventurous pursuit of anything else was pointless; however, for the location of every item in the world laid within the pages of the book before him. His success was turning out to be more destructive than constructive as he began figuring out the tribulations of having every piece of knowledge at his fingertips. Nothing was a mystery and knowledge of everything was encompassed by the book before him. One question bore deep into Braxton's mind: *What is one to do when he has found the answer to everything?*

The answer to this question was quite obvious: nothing. Everything was without meaning and the intrigue had been stripped from his life like color being removed from his very surroundings. Due to the book, everything was like black and white, for it is impossible to learn or be surprised when every fact and trick known to man was a page away. Maybe the book was right about itself. It didn't pose a danger to the rest of the world now, but it seemed to be setting its sights on destroying Braxton's sense of creativity and adventure. When one allows their life to become devoid of fascination and curiosity, everything becomes a drab and dull misery.

As he came to the realization of his predicament, Braxton asked the *Book of Knowledge* one final question. The pages ruffled once more as the book thought up an answer to give the prying eyes of its captor. All that was written on the page was the following simple reply, "In a world full of darkness, you have finally truly seen the light." At this moment, Braxton had a thought he'd never had before. Perhaps his aims of trying to control his fate were fruitless as all that Braxton truly had to do was reap the contentment from today and allow tomorrow to come as it was. It was senseless to obsess and fuss over tomorrow if it cost him today. All he was doing was cheating himself of today by fantasizing and wishing for the days to come. He had to live for the day he was living. He could never do such a feat with the book leeching the enjoyment of not knowing from his life.

Staring out into the bleakness of night, an answer came to Braxton that was not provided by the book before him. Braxton's solution to this conundrum was to simply put the book away. He'd hide it out of sight from the next unknowing adventurer who would seek it out next in hopes of it solving all their problems and mistakes. Perhaps he could save another man from the dangers of his own success. If the book was uncovered again, its finder would surely come to the same realization that Braxton had. After stowing the book in the bottom drawer of his desk, Braxton shut and locked the compartment. If he ever needed the book's assistance, it was there, but it would burden his conscience no longer with its wisdom and worldliness. Braxton was free from the clutches of his prize.

The world itself was an open book that Braxton was not quite ready to put down yet. There was still much to be seen and much to be done. Braxton decided that he would do something that, at one time, he'd never imagined he'd even humor or consider in his life. He'd travel the world and simply go out and find what was out there to be seen. There was no place for business trips or long-term itineraries in his life anymore. All that was left to do was for Braxton to go out and live for today. Despite this sudden burst of ambition, the hour was getting late as the moon had crested in the star-filled sky. Braxton was tired and drained from his chaotic day of sailing across a channel, potentially saving the world, and being trampled by his personal revelations of life. Braxton finished his scotch and decided that it was best that he get himself to bed before any further pangs of guilt or regret rattled him further. As he settled in beneath his sheets and adjusted his pillow, Braxton knew that this was not the end of everything he had ever known to this point in his life. It was merely the end to a beginning that would surely be followed by another chapter that Braxton was ready to savor one day at a time.

When Braxton awoke, the sun had just begun to rise in the eastern sky, that was streaked with red, orange, and yellow ripples that marked the light of a new day. Braxton fixed himself a breakfast of eggs, bacon, and toast. He also fetched himself a warm glass of apple cider from the cellar to compliment his breakfast and fight off the bitter cold of the winter morning. These simple pleasures were all that Braxton needed to be content in that very moment. After finishing his breakfast, Braxton went upstairs to his study to evaluate the aftermath of last night. Everything was exactly where he put it, for better or worse. A disorderly array of papers and journals were scattered across the floor by the desk where Braxton had swept them off to make room for the *Book of Knowledge*. Once he'd picked up his papers, he moderately organized them back to their state of orderly chaos that they were in before. Braxton somehow knew where everything was on his desk, regardless of how buried it was. The next thing that Braxton did was ensure that the desk drawer that was holding the *Book of Knowledge* was actually locked by tugging at the handle. After a couple of tries for good measure, the drawer remained sealed and locked, shielding the evil that lay within it from the light of day. Braxton sat in his desk chair once more and just took the sunset in from his study's window. His view was impeccable for something that was ignored and taken for granted by him for so long. He could see for miles as the rolling hills and groves of trees seemed to stretch to infinity. The simple pleasures in life are often the most overlooked and the last to be appreciated.

As the sunrise dwindled in grandeur, Braxton found his mind wandering to the places he'd been in the last few weeks. He'd seemingly seen every dale, harbor, and hillside in the entire Great Expanse as his wagon had rumbled down every dusty trail that was offered to wandering travelers. Braxton was curious as to what would happen to Pierce's estate, but he figured his creditors would either pick the place apart looking to reclaim their losses or sell it off to another pompous aristocrat who would carry on the tradition of being generously awful to the people of Merchant's Grove.

The earth continued to spin regardless of what mortal tragedies burdened its inhabitants. City streets continued to bustle and come alive with the same crowds, regardless of their overseers. Injustices and good deeds continued to happen simultaneously, despite the

160

oversight of whatever higher power lingered in the heavens. Everything kept moving forward.

Braxton had come to terms with the fact that the world was both a cruel and wonderful place to be. For every upside, there was a downside. For every sunny day, there was a period of pouring rain that would soon follow. For every person that had found their passion in their calling, there were millions still venturing towards their own conclusions. Life is a series of contrasting concepts that help bring the whole journey together through its intricacies and novelties.

Contentment was the game, and life was simply the effort put forth to become a victor of the game. Everybody was looking for something, and it was certainly somewhere out there for them to grasp. Braxton was eager to go find his piece of contentment, but for right now, he was satisfied cooped up in his study, pondering the philosophies and possibilities of the life ahead of him. His train of vivid thought was interrupted when he heard a knock on the door downstairs. The last visitor that had paid him a visit was Pierce, so Braxton had high hopes that whoever was at his door was more pleasant than the late aristocrat. As Braxton walked downstairs, he wondered who had paid him a visit this quickly after the events of the previous day, for it surely wasn't James as he was more than likely still figuring himself out. The curiosity was something that built both anticipation and a morsel of fear for what awaited the man outside his front door. As far as he could see through the small window in his door, nobody stood directly in front of his stoop. Braxton had no patience for practical jokesters or elusive door-to-door salesmen. He opened the door to be greeted by no one. After a brief moment of confusion, Braxton looked down to find something peculiar laying on the ground. A familiar silver pocket watch gleamed in the sunlight on a white handkerchief.

About the Author

Knolan Kemp is a young writer who began writing *The Philosopher* at the age of seventeen while finishing his senior year of high school. As an avid learner and curious mind, Knolan enjoys listening to classic rock, reading other novels, and traveling. He was born and raised in southwestern Wisconsin where he currently resides. Woven throughout his writings are fragments and pieces of knowledge and references that have greatly influenced him as a writer and as an individual. *The Philosopher* is the first book by Knolan Kemp.

Printed in the USA
CPSIA information can be obtained
at www.ICGtesting.com
LVHW091304131023
760665LV00003B/506